When Tasker overhears a few bonded gargoyles and their mates planning a night out at a strip club, he convinces them to sneak him in through the back. Once there, to Tasker's shock, he scents his mate somewhere in the seedy joint. With a little help from friends, Tasker discovers that a sexy black stripper with the stage name Mongo is his mate. The human's medium-brown skin and bleached-blond hair calls to him, but as much as Tasker would love to whisk the human from the place, he knows that wouldn't be a good move . . . so he once again relies on friends.

Camry Palcha never thought he would end up a stripper, but after getting cut off when he came out, desperate times calls for desperate measures. The pay is good, even though he refuses the side offers of backroom hook-ups with clients. While he'll never admit it to anyone at the seedy place, he's a virgin. No way does he want his first time to be with someone paying him.

When a guy named Mitch approaches Camry about hiring him for a private gig, he nearly refuses. Except, the money will set him up for months, and that's after covering his upcoming college tuition. When Camry arrives at the address, he's shocked to find himself at a mansion. After girding up his courage and entering, Camry learns that paranormals are real. When one comes onto him, Camry has no experience to fall back on. Could Tasker's interest truly be real? Or was the gargoyle's desire simply a novelty, just like the rich jerks at the strip club who've been pestering Camry for weeks?

The Gargoyle and the Stripper
Copyright © 2022 Charlie Richards
ISBN: 978-1-4874-3618-6
Cover art by Angela Waters

Published by eXtasy Books Inc

Look for us online at:
www.eXtasybooks.com

The Gargoyle and the Stripper
A Paranormal's Love: Book Thirty-Seven

By

Charlie Richards

CHAPTER ONE

"The place ain't high-class or anything, but if you wanna check out strippers, it's the closest."

Tasker overheard Mitch's words as he walked past the dining hall table containing the human and a bunch of his friends. Carrying his tray of food in one hand, he paused and took a sip of the coffee in his other hand. That allowed him to continue eavesdropping on the four humans seated at the table.

"Why are we talking about going to a strip club again?" Aaden asked dryly, smirking at Mitch.

It was a valid question. All four of the humans—Mitch, Aaden, Andre, and Aziel—were mated to paranormals. The first three to gargoyles, and the final man to a giant otter shifter.

Shrugging, Mitch grinned. "'Cause my man says if I wanna see some titties, I can. I just don't touch anymore," he stated, referring to his mate, Kardamon.

From what Tasker had heard, Kardamon had had a tough time of seducing Mitch. The human had been a bit of a womanizer. He'd enjoyed the bed of a different female every few evenings, and he'd always made certain they knew the score—he wouldn't keep any of them. With the help of Mitch's friends, Kardamon had convinced Mitch to not only accept a male lover, but that bonding and tying himself to him would make him happy.

Gods, I hope I don't have to work that hard for my own mate . . . whenever I find him or her, anyway.

"Plus," Mitch continued, pointing at Aziel. "I heard your

1

brother is coming to town, and he just separated from his cheating bitch of a wife." With a snort, he lifted his hands wide as if the answer was obvious. "What a perfect way to cheer him up!"

"Uh." Aziel rubbed his large black hand over his jaw, his uncertainty clear. "I'm not sure Aaron's into that sort of thing, but I can ask him."

"Naw, don't bother to ask," Mitch countered. "It'll be a surprise. A guy's night out. He'll love it."

Aziel didn't appear completely convinced, but he did nod slowly.

"Awesome." Mitch patted him on one huge shoulder before turning to the others. "Well? Come on then, guys." His tone turned wheedling. "You have to. It'll be a fun night of eye candy. Then we can all go home and fuck like bunnies."

"We fuck like bunnies anyway," Andre commented with a chuckle.

Mitch laughed. "So." The man rose from the table, having clearly finished his food—and convincing his friends of his plan—and began placing all his wrappers on his tray. "Let's go talk to the guys. Should we invite anyone else?"

Recalling another part of Kardamon's task of seducing Mitch, Tasker made a snap decision. "Hey, guys." He grinned at the four young men—two who were still in college to get master's degrees. "I couldn't help but overhear your conversation."

"Hey, Tasker," Mitch greeted, returning his toothy smile. He waggled his brows and asked, "How's it hangin'?"

Tasker quipped back, "Straight down, at the moment, but I bet it'll be straight up if you can talk Kardamon into sneaking me in with you guys. When are you going?"

Kardamon had managed to sneak into the strip joint to confront Mitch while in the process of seducing him. If the big blue gargoyle could get in, surely Tasker could, too. While

Tasker was also blue, although a paler shade, he was much smaller than his hulking fellow gargoyle and could blend in with humans much easier.

Well, that was what he guessed, anyway.

"You want to come?" Mitch sounded surprised. When Tasker nodded, the human's brows furrowed. "When Kardamon went there, he couldn't like . . . touch or like . . . interact much."

Tasker shrugged before using his coffee mug to point at the four guys, who were all eyeing him with open curiosity. "Then I'll be just like you all. Just there to watch." He offered them a wry smile as he added, "I just won't be planning on fucking like bunnies when I get home."

"Twilden still upset with you?" Aziel murmured softly in his deep voice. His brows were furrowed in a slight grimace.

Sighing deeply, Tasker nodded. "Yeah." The small gargoyle was one of his usual fuck-buddies but had been refusing to give him the time of day after he'd made a thoughtless comment to him. "And Beldrew has refused me, too, after talking with Twilden." Tasker grimaced, hunching his shoulders, as he muttered, "Can't say as I blame them, though."

Aziel patted Tasker on the shoulder in commiseration. "It's never a good idea to compare dick sizes of your fuck buddies."

Tipping his head back, Tasker groaned. "I know," he whined. "I'd just come, and we were lying together, and . . . I just blurted it out."

Tasker had known it was wrong to compare the two gargoyles' dicks the second the words were out of his throat. He didn't blame the pair for being pissed at him. While gargoyles — and most paranormals — weren't monogamous until finding their mates, they did have a high sex drive. For his two regular fuck-buddies to be refusing him, Tasker was getting real friendly with his right hand, and he was getting tired of it.

"Maybe we can figure out a way for you to make it up to them," Aaden offered, picking up his own dish-laden tray.

"Thanks," Tasker replied. The humans really were a good group of guys. Smirking, he added, "But after the strip club. When are you planning to go, anyway?"

"My brother, Aaron, will be here tomorrow," Aziel revealed, also grabbing his own tray. "He's staying at a bed and breakfast in town." After a sigh, he admitted, "I petitioned Chieftain Maelgwn to bring him here and let him in on paranormals, considering our upbringing, but I'm not sure if he'll allow it."

"Well, tomorrow is Thursday," Mitch pointed out. "So, we'll give him a night to recover from his drive from Colorado Springs." With a nod, Mitch stated, "We'll go to the strip club on Friday night." Mitch laughed. "I bet the place will be jumpin'." He patted Tasker's upper arm. "I'll go talk to Kardamon right now."

Tasker nodded. "Thanks, man."

Mitch gave him a thumbs up. Then all the guys moved toward the counter to throw away their garbage and place their dirty dishes in the assorted bins. After a final wave from each of them, they headed out of the dining hall.

Tasker grinned to himself as he carried his tray out another door. He'd been the last in the room and would rather sit alone on the roof rather than in the hall. It'd taken him longer to dice up the huge vat of potatoes Roman—their clutch's head chef—had needed prepped for a number of ham and potato casseroles he intended to make.

Heading out one of the massive estate's back doors, Tasker spread his wings, bent his knees, and jumped into the air. He flapped his large white wings several times and caught an air current. Rising toward the dark sky, Tasker winged his way onto the roof.

Halfway through his meal, Tasker heard the sound of another gargoyle's wingbeats. He lowered his second double-bacon cheeseburger and peered to his left. When Tasker spotted Chieftain Maelgwn, tension ratcheted through him.

Is my chieftain about to declare that I can't go out with the guys?

From what had been whispered through the grapevine, Kardamon hadn't asked permission at the time. Of course, the gargoyle was a guard and had experience with turning humans away from their property without revealing their existence. Tasker mainly worked in the kitchens, as well as handling a few other mundane — but necessary — household tasks.

Plus, Kardamon hadn't gotten himself into trouble just a few months prior.

Tasker had made the mistake of propositioning another gargoyle, Holden, while in a room they were prepping for a visitor from another clutch. When Holden had opened his mouth, most likely to turn him down — Tasker had been able to see it in the other gargoyle's eyes — he hadn't gotten the chance to speak. Second Tobias had walked in right then with their clutch's guest, a vampire named Lathe. Suffice it to say, Tobias had been livid. It hadn't helped that Lathe had ended up being Holden's mate. Understandably, Holden had left their clutch to join Lathe's.

"Hi, Tasker," Chieftain Maelgwn greeted, landing a few feet to his left. His smile appeared warm, and there was no hint of ire in his scent, which helped Tasker to relax. When the chieftain waved at his food and added, "Please, don't stop on my account," Tasker relaxed a little more.

"Good evening, Chieftain," Tasker replied. Before bringing the burger back to his lips, he asked, "How can I be of service?"

Maelgwn scoffed softly as he slowly lowered himself to a nearby bench seat placed on the roof. "Just checking in to see how you're doing," the chieftain stated, surprising Tasker. Before he could chew and swallow his bite, Maelgwn continued, "The clutch has gone through an unprecedented event . . . so many of us finding our mates. But that change brings difficulties, too." His expression sobered as he leaned forward, resting his forearms on his thighs. "Especially for those who haven't yet been one of the blessed."

Tasker set down his burger and picked up his coffee, trying to decide what would be an acceptable response. Taking a sip, he bought himself time to think.

Smiling, perhaps recognizing the stalling tactic for what it was, Maelgwn stated, "I just want to make certain you're still happy here, Tasker." He threaded his dark blue fingers together as he held him in a steady gaze. "And, please, don't think I'm singling you out just because of your recent past. I'm asking all the remaining single gargoyles these questions." After a second of hesitation, Maelgwn offered, "If you'd be more comfortable in a clutch with fewer bonded couples, then I'll do everything in my power to find one that you'll be happy in."

"I don't want to leave," Tasker blurted, shaking his head. Surprise surged through him. "Please." Hesitating, he tried to figure out how to express himself. Tasker went with, "Yes, seeing all these couples together is sometimes difficult. But it also gives me hope." After setting down his coffee mug, Tasker rubbed his chest absently. "Hope that Fate will bless me soon."

Lifting his hands, palms out in obvious placation, Maelgwn rumbled, "Relax, Tasker. I would never send any of my people away without cause." He lowered his hands and smiled. "And I pray that your mate will appear soon enough." Scoffing, Maelgwn added, "All of the mates for my remaining single gargoyles. You all should be so blessed as to have found what your fellow clutch mates have."

"Thank you, Chieftain," Tasker replied, relief flooding him. He picked up his burger again. "I look forward to that day, and until then, I'll strive to continue to do my duties to you and this clutch."

Maelgwn nodded, an easy smile curving his lips. "I'm glad to hear it." Then his lips widened into a shit-eating grin. "Now, what's this I hear about the guys sneaking you into a strip club?"

"Uhhhh . . ."

His chieftain laughed.

Tasker couldn't believe it. He was actually sitting inside a strip club surrounded by unknowledgeable humans. Of course, with the way Tasker was dressed, no one would approach him. Not to mention that he was sandwiched in the middle of a large, curved booth.

Aaden, with a grumpy-looking Grigoris, sat to his left, while Mitch and Kardamon sat on his right. In a nearby booth, Aziel sat with his brother, Aaron, and his own mate, Jerome. With them were Andre and his gargoyle mate, Sumak.

Scattered around the place were a few other members of the clutch, with their mates, who'd been curious about the place.

Staring at the main stage, Tasker watched a voluptuous woman with long red hair dance using a pole. As he admired her flexibility, he wondered what it would be like to bed a woman who could move like that. Tasker hadn't sunk his cock into a female in nearly . . .

Damn. It must have been nearly one hundred and fifty years.

Tasker smiled, thinking about the sister of one of the mated gargoyles in his prior clutch. She'd found out about paranormals by accident but had taken it in stride. The woman had found their colors fascinating, and she'd had great fun in sleeping with a male of every color.

And I was happy to help her experiment.

7

"Thinking about the redhead? Or someone else?" Mitch teased, nudging him with his elbow. He even waggled his eyebrows suggestively. "She does have really nice tits." Then Mitch wrinkled his nose as he added, "Seen her disappear into the back with customers a time or two." He shook his head as he muttered, "Never could figure out the allure of paying for sex."

"And you never will have to worry about that again," Kardamon stated on a growl. His dark eyes were narrowed as he pinned a hungry look on Mitch. "You're mine."

Mitch smirked and patted Kardamon's hand. "You know it, big guy."

"Just thinking about the last woman I bedded," Tasker admitted, answering Mitch's question. With a chuckle, he admitted, "It was a long time ago, and she—" The smell of something earthy and masculine floated across Tasker's senses, distracting him. "What's that?" Unable to help himself, he flicked out his tongue, trying to get a better read on the scent.

"What are you doing?" Grigoris growled, frowning at him as he leaned closer. "Can't do that in here, Tasker."

"Sorry," Tasker replied on reflex. "Just . . . there's something in the air here, and I—"

The tantalizing aroma wafted by him again, and he felt his blood stir in a way that had absolutely nothing to do with the stripper who'd just finished her routine. He ignored her and her bare breasts, which were on clear display as she strutted off stage. Instead, Tasker was too busy peering around the place, trying to discern the airways in the too-warm establishment.

Except, the sweat that beaded on Tasker's swarthy hide beneath his clothing had nothing to do with the temperature. He practically vibrated with the need to get up and walk around. His dick, which had only been at half-mast, thickened and swelled, becoming decidedly uncomfortable within the confines of his jeans.

Gripping the edge of the table, Tasker barely managed to keep from sinking his claws through the thick fabric of the leather gloves he wore. If he scored the table, it would be pretty hard to explain to the waiter, who was supposed to be returning soon with their second round of drinks.

"Talk to us, Tasker," Grigoris demanded forcefully, although quietly. The gargoyle was their clutch's mechanic, but he was also an enforcer when needed, and he had the dominant personality to match. When Grigoris gripped Tasker's shoulder and ordered, "Tell me what's wrong," he wouldn't have been able to deny him even if he'd wanted to.

Plus, Tasker didn't, as the reason for his reaction hit his suddenly lust-addled brain.

"My mate is somewhere in here."

"Well, holy shit," Mitch muttered, glancing around as if that person would suddenly appear at their table. "Who?"

Staring wide-eyed at Mitch, Tasker shook his head. "I-I don't know."

"Don't worry." Kardamon patted his shoulder. "Just keep it together. We'll figure it out."

Tasker nodded as his mouth began to water from a fresh wash of the scent flowing over his senses.

Damn it. Where is it coming from?

Chapter Two

Rolling his head on his neck, Camry Palcha slowly stretched in preparation for his set. He could hear the cheers for Samantha — stage name Fireball in deference to her flaming red hair. Camry stood backstage in front of the vents, enjoying the last bit of cool air flowing over his skin.

Camry knew that soon, his dark skin would be gleaming for a reason other than the oil he'd slathered on his body. Unbeknownst to a lot of people, working a pole while stripping was a full-body exercise. After his three evening sets, his muscles would be exhausted.

It doesn't help that I was supposed to have tonight off so I helped a neighbor move a couple of pieces of furniture.

Unfortunately, Carlton Withers — the sleazy owner of the place — had ordered him to come in.

And ordered was right. Instead of asking if Camry was available, he'd called and demanded him. When Camry had pointed out that Fridays catered to the male crowd, not the female, his boss had assured him that his routine . . . and his presence . . . would be well appreciated.

Camry really hadn't liked that insinuation, but he needed his job. So, he'd shown up.

"And now, here by popular request, a performance that the ladies in the crowd will certainly appreciate," Carlton cried, causing a number of cheers to rent the air. "Give a warm round of applause for Mongo!"

Popular request? Shit! God, I hope it's not who I think it is.

Camry sauntered forward, keeping his limbs loose and his

movements sensual as he strutted onto the stage. He pushed those thoughts from his mind. While he knew the stage lights highlighted him and his body, they made it difficult to peer into the booths that surrounded the room. Camry didn't bother trying.

Hell, I don't want to know.

Instead, Camry focused on the music that began piping through the sound system. He allowed it to flow through him, and he began to move. His body responded easily, slipping into the choreographed moves as he grabbed the pole and started to dance.

Allowing his eyes to slide to half-mast and his lips to curve into a half-smile, Camry focused on nothing but the dance. He'd been told that his expression made him appear even more sensual, but that hadn't been the purpose when he'd first adopted it several months before. Instead, it was so he didn't have to focus on the lustful looks and heated gazes of those pressing close to the stage. Although, Camry certainly appreciated the cash they threw at him.

Gotta pay the rent somehow, and it certainly ain't gonna be from accepting backroom hook-ups from some of the clientele.

No matter how rich they are or how much they ask.

Demanded, more like, recently.

In Camry's peripheral vision, he noted where the bills fell. He needed that information to know where to bow at the end of his performance. Camry also needed to know so he didn't accidentally step on one and slip.

Yeah, that would be a performance killer.

By the time Camry finished, having removed three pairs of thongs as if he were really going to show off his package, sweat dripped from his body. He picked up one of them and threw it into the crowd of cheering women, as he waved, just because it was expected. Plus, Carlton always supplied plenty of thongs.

Huh. There are some men off to the left cheering, too. Guess they're not all straights tonight.

After taking several bows, collecting his underwear and cash along the way, Camry made his way back into the dressing room. He quickly rubbed himself down, removing oil and sweat in equal measure. Donning the short-shorts and tank top Carlton ordered as his uniform, Camry prepared to mingle for his required half an hour before he could escape back into the dressing rooms.

Carlton claimed it brought in more money if the customers could interact with the object of their infatuation.

Camry hated it because all it really did was give them an opportunity to paw at him.

Dick.

Cramming those dark thoughts to the back of his mind, Camry shoved his feet into a pair of low-heeled boots that matched the shorts. He took a deep breath before gripping the doorknob. After releasing it slowly, he headed out to the floor.

Doing his best to avoid too-appreciative hands, Camry circled the floor. He kept his grin pasted on his face as he talked with fans. Mostly, he just thanked the people for their compliments about how stunning he was on stage.

When Camry had first started the job, he'd realized very quickly that he was relegated to an object in most people's minds. They saw him and thought of him as something pretty to lust after. That was after he made the mistake of accepting a date from one of the regulars.

It had been the worst night of Camry's life. The man had taken him out to dinner, where he'd talked all about himself, asking nothing about Camry. Then he'd asked him to come home with him and give him a private show.

Yep. So not happening.

Camry glanced toward the clock, hoping his half-hour was up. Relief filled him when he realized he only had two more minutes to go. He began sidling in the direction of the back, declining an offer of a drink from a nearby patron.

"Come and have a drink with me, instead, Mongo."

Hearing the words and recognizing the voice, Camry did his best not to cringe. He couldn't help the flinch when he felt a cold hand wrap around his upper arm. He felt the client tug, and he resisted the urge to yank away from the guy.

Camry forced himself to appear flattered as he met the other man's cold, gray-eyed gaze. "I'm sorry, Mister Clarence," he countered with a slight shake of his head. "I have one more set this evening. I can't drink at work."

While Camry had noticed other dancers accept people's offers, he refused to be one of them. He needed his wits about him in a seedy place such as this. If he hadn't needed the job so badly, no way would he have worked there.

Mister Clarence's grip tightened a smidge. "I know that's not the rule," he countered, his eyes narrowing in obvious warning. "And I'm certain I've told you to call me Morgan."

"I'm flattered, Mister Clarence," Camry lied. "It's a personal rule. It's dangerous to dance after drinking."

"Just one drink, then." Morgan again tried to guide him toward a booth off to the side. "I've already ordered it. It won't take long."

Oh, hell no!

If the drink was already waiting at the table, there was no telling what Morgan could have slipped into it.

Rich assholes think they can get whatever they want.

"Hey, Camry." A jovial voice filled the air as Camry felt someone sling an arm over his shoulders. "So glad I caught you before you returned to the back." The dark-haired man grinned broadly at Morgan. "You don't mind if I borrow my buddy for a minute, do you, man? I know he's gotta get back to work soon."

Evidently, the fact that the guy had used Camry's given name created enough uncertainty in Morgan that his grip loosened. That allowed the stranger to pull Camry from him. He immediately turned Camry and began guiding him away.

13

Glancing over the dark-haired man for a second before meeting his blue eyes, Camry muttered, "Uh, thanks, but who are you?"

"M'name's Mitch," he told him with a wide grin. Waggling his eyebrows, he added, "Don't worry, man. I'm not after your hot bod." He jerked his chin toward the right, indicating someone in one of the booths over there. "Got my own hot man right over there." Then Mitch's brows furrowed as he added, "But that dude kinda gave me the creeps."

"Yeah. Me, too," Camry admitted. "Normally, I can avoid him." Realizing what he'd just admitted to a stranger, he stumbled, "Um, I mean, I—"

"Eh, don't sweat it," Mitch countered with a chuckle. "I get what you mean." His blue eyes danced with mischief as he added, "And your secret is safe with me." Then Mitch's gaze turned speculative as he continued, "Look, this is probably really bad form, but I have to ask . . . do you ever do private shows?"

Camry opened his mouth once, then closed it again. Surprise flooded him, even though he'd been asked for private shows before. That had been the last thing he would have guessed the astute guy would have asked.

He just hadn't seemed like the type, and Camry had gotten pretty good at recognizing them.

Lifting his free hand in obvious placation, Mitch told him, "It's not for me," he quickly told him. "It's for my friend. He's a recluse, but I know he would really love your vibe." Offering him a lopsided smile, Mitch added, "The pay would be fantastic, and you wouldn't have to worry about any grabby hands. Promise."

Glancing around, Camry found himself tempted for the first time in . . . ever. He spotted Carlton staring at him with narrowed eyes. Clearing his throat, Camry returned his attention to Mitch.

Camry tipped his face close to Mitch's, so he could whisper into his ear. At the same time, he pinned a suggestive look on his face. As he spoke, he knew anyone looking would think he was saying something provocative to the other man.

"I really can't talk about outside jobs while working," Camry murmured to Mitch. "Carlton, my boss, will insist on a cut if I pick up a side job while here."

Mitch, obviously catching on, grinned while tilting his head so he could whisper right back. "How about I give you my phone number, and you can call me?" He even moved his arm away from his shoulder so he could squeeze his upper arm. "We can talk about the deets."

"Okay," Camry found himself agreeing.

After all, I don't actually have to call him if I decide not to.

Sliding his hand into his pocket, Mitch pulled out a twenty-dollar bill and a pen. He quickly wrote his number on it, then held it out to Camry while saying, "Your show was fantastic, Camry. Better than most of the women's."

"Thanks. It's normally lost on the guys," Camry admitted.

Mitch grinned broadly and shrugged his wide shoulders. "The group of guys I'm with are all bi." Then he added with a wink, "And most are in committed relationships, but we enjoy a little eye candy now and again." After one more pat to Camry's shoulder, Mitch stated, "Talk to you soon."

Then Mitch turned and headed in the direction he'd earlier indicated with his chin.

Spotting Carlton headed his way, Camry pretended he didn't and hurried into the back. He knew that wouldn't stop his boss from questioning him, but at least he wouldn't have to deal with it in public. Just as Camry had suspected, Carlton followed him into his dressing room.

"Who was that?" Carlton demanded. "He seemed friendly, and he interrupted your time with Mister Clarence." Crossing his arms over his pudgy chest, he confirmed Camry's suspicions by saying, "Mister Clarence requested you here tonight because he's out of town tomorrow. You need to be a little more attentive to our higher-paying clients."

Camry feigned surprise. "Oh, I'm sorry, Mister Withers. The guy introduced himself as Mitch." He waved the bill he'd been handed and tossed that as well as the others he'd picked up while mingling onto the table. "Just a fan who liked the way I danced." Rubbing his jaw, Camry shifted his weight from foot to foot as he told the man, "Asked me on a date, but, uh, I don't date white guys."

While that was total bullshit—Camry didn't care what a guy looked like so much as how he acted—he hoped it would be a good cover. Besides, Mister Clarence was white, too. Maybe if Camry tossed that ridiculous fact out there, his boss would stop trying to pimp him out to the rich asshole.

Carlton's next words told Camry he wasn't that lucky.

"Well, after your last set, make sure you sit down and have that drink with Mister Clarence," Carlton ordered, scowling at the pile of cash. His pudgy fingers twitched as if he wanted to take some—or all—of it.

Most likely, he did.

"Yes, sir," Camry replied dutifully.

God, this is going to suck.

"You're on in thirty. Get ready," Carlton ordered. After a grunt as he pivoted, plus another look at Camry's tips, his boss left the room.

Just in case Carlton returned during Camry's final set—or after while having that drink with Morgan Clarence—Camry sifted through the pile and pulled out the larger bills. Those, he neatly folded and hid in the false bottom of his duffle bag. He left the pile of ones and fives on his dressing table.

After his final set, Camry did as he'd been ordered. He sought out Morgan Clarence. First, however, he picked up a bottle of water from the bar.

When Morgan offered to get him something stronger,

Camry smiled sweetly and told him, "Oh, no, thank you, sir. I need to rehydrate."

Camry knew Morgan didn't like his answer, but he didn't press the issue.

Camry also didn't release the bottle from his hand the entire time he sat at the table and listened to the dick share about his vast wealth.

Whatever. Money is only as good as its ability to keep a roof over my head.

Before long, Camry didn't need to fake his yawns. He apologized and made his excuses. As Camry hurried to the back to change once more, he felt the hairs on his nape stand on end, and he just knew Morgan was watching him.

As Camry drove his old *Ford* sedan home, he kept glancing over his shoulder. He didn't see anyone, but as he entered his apartment building, he could have sworn he still felt as if he was being watched.

With a sigh, Camry locked himself into his one-bedroom apartment. He leaned his back against the wood and let out a long sigh.

"Just damn," Camry muttered. "How did my life come to this?"

Camry didn't wait for an answer from the cosmos. After all, he already knew. He'd foolishly thought that his parents wouldn't care that he was gay.

They had . . . and they'd cut him off.

Utilizing his years of contemporary dance lessons, Camry had decided the stripper gig wouldn't be too bad. He just had to dance nearly naked in front of people. Having never been to a strip club himself, Camry hadn't anticipated the seediness of the place.

Maybe they weren't all like that, but now Camry was stuck. If he wanted to continue to pay for college classes, even part-time as he was currently doing, he needed the job. Camry hadn't found anything he was qualified for that paid as much.

Pushing away from the door, Camry began his evening clean-up routine.

Late the next morning, Camry stared at the twenty-dollar bill and the phone number written on it. He'd been contemplating what to do all morning. Finally, he'd decided it wouldn't hurt to call Mitch and find out the specifics of the offer.

CHAPTER THREE

"**I** told him no grabby hands," Mitch warned. "So you'll need to get permission to touch."

Tasker immediately nodded. "I know. I will."

Mitch had only warned him half a dozen times or so.

I'm beginning to think he doesn't trust me.

After figuring out who gave off the alluring scent in the strip club, Tasker had needed every ounce of self-control—as well as the grip Grigoris had on his thigh under the table—to keep from whisking the sexy human right the hell out of there.

So, yeah. I guess I can understand why Mitch may not trust me.

Tasker glanced at the clock, and unease slithered up his spine. "He's late."

"Uh, actually, he's sitting at the front gate." Mitch was staring at his phone, which had gone off a few seconds prior with a text alert. Grimacing, he flipped the phone around to show the screen to Tasker. "I think he might be a little intimidated."

Taking the offered device, Tasker peered at the picture on the phone. He realized it was a live video feed from one of their front gate's security cameras. The screen showed an older model *Ford* sedan stopped at the control box. Considering the window had been rolled down, Tasker saw that Camry had his arm partly out the window, as if reaching to hit the buzzer. Except, he sat frozen, staring at the huge gates with a wide-eyed gaze.

As Tasker watched, Second Tobias's voice came through, indicating that he was speaking through the call box. "Hello,

Camry," he greeted in a soft rumble, probably recognizing the deer in the headlights look that Camry sported. "You're expected. Won't you come in?"

Then . . . the gates began to roll open.

"I—" Camry's voice came out with a little bit of a squeak to it, and he paused a second. Then he swallowed hard enough that, even through the camera, Tasker could see Camry's Adam's apple bob. "Uh, yes. Thank you."

With the warmth of the evening, Camry wore a short-sleeved shirt, showing off his dark skin and muscular limb, which he pulled back into the car. He sucked in a deep breath before blowing it out through full dark lips. After rubbing a hand over his closely-cropped, bleached-blond hair, his dark-skinned mate put the vehicle into gear, and he started forward.

Tasker's anticipation ramped up.

Soon. Soon I'll be able to see my mate again.

Two nights before, Tasker had followed Camry home from the strip club. He'd been grateful for the tree-lined road, which had made it simple to fly near his car without being seen. Once on the outskirts of town, Tasker had switched to using the rooftops.

Tasker had been surprised to see Camry enter an older apartment building that often catered to struggling college kids and single parents. The place was on the poorer end of town, and many people there relied on the bus system.

As much as Tasker wanted to camp out there the prior evening, too, his chieftain had encouraged him not to. Instead, he'd had Raymond do a deep search on the man. Tasker had read everything Raymond had sent about him at least three times. He'd stared at the pictures for so long, he felt certain he'd memorized every facet of his mate's features.

And now, soon, I'll meet him in person.

Tasker hoped his human took the paranormal reveal well. According to what Raymond had dug up on him, he no longer had any contact with his family. That would make bringing him into the fold so much easier — no ties to cling to.

"Okay." Mitch took his phone back from Tasker and patted him on the shoulder. "Sit tight. I'm going to go get him."

After nodding, Tasker began pacing the room. He glanced around the space. When he'd prepared it, he'd hoped to set his mate up with a relaxing atmosphere in which to learn about paranormals.

To that end, Tasker had chosen one of the estate's smaller recreation and lounging areas. There was a bar at the end, which was fully stocked. There was a pool table, a ping-pong table, a foosball table, and a huge TV mounted on one wall with plenty of comfortable sofas and chairs of various sizes.

There was not, however, a place for Camry to change or a stripper pole. The second his mate walked into the room, he would know that he'd been lured there for ulterior purposes. Tasker sure hoped the mate-pull would work quickly in his favor.

I've seen it happen with others. Everything will be fine.

"Hey, try to relax," Grigoris urged, resting his hand on Tasker's shoulder and ceasing his pacing. "By Fate's will, everything will work out fine." Then the big mechanic released him and pointed toward the French doors leading to an expansive back patio which transitioned into the estate's sprawling gardens. "Go face the doors and drape your wings around you. Let's not freak him out as soon as he walks in the room. Hmm?"

Tasker nodded, seeing the wisdom in that. Plus, even with nerves running through his system, his cock was hard as nails in anticipation. He wanted to feel his mate against his own body in the worst way.

As Tasker stared out into the night with his white wings draped over his shoulders, he thought about what his human's smooth dark skin would feel like. From watching it gleam in the club light as he twisted around the pole, he guessed it to feel smooth and hairless. The hard ass muscles had flexed enticingly, on clear display due to the thong he'd worn, and Tasker wanted to cradle and squeeze them.

They'll be the perfect handfuls as I —

"Get your head out of the gutter, Tasker."

Chieftain Maelgwn's voice sounded behind him. When Tasker snapped open eyelids he didn't even remember closing, he used the glass to peer at his smirking chieftain. Even with Maelgwn in his human form, the six-foot-five male towered over Tasker's six-foot-one height.

Tasker was considered short for a gargoyle of his kind — the ones who had wings sprouting from their back as opposed to those like Raymond and Sumak, with wingskins and bone-spurs.

"Chieftain," Tasker responded in surprise. "What, uh, what can I do for you?"

Maelgwn arched one dark brow as he stared at him through the glass reflection. "I'm here to offer one of my men congratulations on finding the other half of his soul." His expression softened into a smile as he added, "And to aid him in any way I can so that he may secure his bond."

"Thank you, Chieftain," Tasker replied, sighing gratefully. "I —"

"Here we are, Camry," Mitch stated, announcing their presence. "Just in here."

"You never did tell me how you knew my real name," Camry replied, his voice drawing closer the more he spoke. "No one at work ever calls me anything but Mongo."

Mitch scoffed. "Ah, yeah. That." He followed that up with a snort. "Who the hell comes up with the names for you and the other dancers?" Without waiting for a response, Mitch added, "Because they suck."

Camry grimaced, his expression easy to make out through the mirror-like surface of the French doors. Even that look caused Tasker's pulse to beat a little faster in his chest. Of course, that could also have been due to the fact that his mate's natural clean scent had begun to tease his senses.

"Anyway," Mitch continued. "As you can imagine from the security here, the guys in charge check out everyone invited here. So . . . when I saw your show and shared how much Tasker would love your vibe, my lover sent a message to the tech guys here, and they started digging." Mitch shrugged. "Sorry."

But he didn't sound like it.

"Uh, so you knew who I really was before you even approached me?" Camry asked, his tone holding a definite note of wariness.

"Your name, yeah," Mitch replied, not sounding the least bit shameful. "After you agreed to swing out here, the powers that be did a deeper dive on you." With a roll of his eyes, Mitch curled his lip and muttered, "Had to make certain you were more trustworthy than that scumbag asshole you work for." Then Mitch sneered as he shook his head.

Tasker's sensitive gargoyle hearing picked up Camry's muttered, "Rich people. Shit." A little louder, he murmured, "Um, maybe I should leave." His gaze swept the room, and he must have finally taken in the space—and those who occupied it—for his dark eyes widened. "Uhhhhh . . ."

Mitch clapped him on the shoulder. "No, man. Ya can't leave now. Haven't introduced you to Tasker, yet." Evidently, Mitch must have noticed the worried crease on Camry's black brows, for he added, "Try to relax. No one here'll give you shit about your opinion on richies. Hell, I totally agree." Curling his lip in a sneer, Mitch continued, "My late father was a rich, entitled asshole, and I'm better off rid of him." He continued shaking his head as he added, "He and my mom. Just . . . sometimes, power corrupts."

Clapping his hands, Mitch continued, "Okay, so the first thing you're probably realizing is that you're not actually here for a strip dance."

"Guess that money offer was too good to be true," Camry muttered, grimacing as he rubbed the back of his neck. "The other shoe always drops with rich guys."

"Oh, you're gonna get paid, man." Mitch patted him on the shoulder. "It's just not for your dancing."

"What?" Camry took a step backward, alarm crossing his features as he obviously jumped to the wrong conclusion. "I won't—"

"Gods, way to make Camry feel more at ease, Mitch." Aaden—Grigoris's human mate—cut in, striding forward. "You're totally not helping here." Sticking out his hand, Aaden greeted, "Hi, Camry. I'm Aaden. Thanks for coming. We really appreciate it, and we're not expecting you to have sex with anyone." Then Aaden grinned widely. "Unless you decide you want to, of course."

"O-Okay," Camry replied uncertainly, but he did take Aaden's hand, shaking. "Um. What's going on?"

"Gods, what a loaded question," Chieftain Maelgwn cut in, striding forward slowly. "Hi, Camry. I'm Maelgwn. I own this place with a couple of partners." He indicated the room. "Please know, you are among friends. You're perfectly safe, and no one here would ever harm you."

Camry's dark eyes narrowed. "Um, thanks for that." Grimacing, he added, "But . . . ya know . . . that kind of welcome speech doesn't really instill me with much confidence."

Maelgwn chuckled softly, shoving his hands into the pockets of his jeans. "Sorry about that, Camry." He shrugged. "It's just something we like to get out right up front."

"We?" Camry asked pointedly.

With a slow nod, Maelgwn replied, "Yes. *We.*" His eyes narrowed just a little as his expression turned serious. "We, as in paranormals." Arching a dark brow, Maelgwn asked, "Do you know what that term means?"

Camry hesitated. "Paranormal?" he repeated. When Maelgwn nodded once, Tasker's mate started slowly, "Uh, I suppose that depends on who you ask. I've heard of a number of, um ... *creatures* ... being described as *paranormal*." Camry even lifted his hands to create air quotes.

"Care to name them for me?" Maelgwn pressed.

After licking his thick lips, which left them gleaming and begging for Tasker's kiss—in his opinion—Camry stated, "Uh, werewolves, vampires, witches." He shrugged and added, "I've read a lot of fantasy, so maybe elves or dwarves or warlocks. Anyone who's not strictly human." Once more, Camry made air quotes.

"Hmmm, I'm glad you said some*one* and not some*thing*," Maelgwn replied with a relaxed smile. "Makes you worlds ahead of many humans."

"R-Really?" Camry sounded taken aback. "Th-Then you believe in those, uh, beings?"

"I do," Maelgwn confirmed. Touching his chest, he continued, "For, you see, I am a gargoyle. The chieftain of my gargoyle clutch, as a matter of fact." With his palm up, he indicated several of them around the room. "Many of those in the room are gargoyles, although there are humans and others thrown in, too."

"Wow," Camry whispered, his brows drawing together.

Camry glanced around the room again, his attention holding on Tasker for a few extra seconds that caused Tasker's heart to beat even faster. From the way Tasker was standing, he knew that Camry couldn't make out anything of him except his white wings and hair. A sofa stood between them, hiding his blue legs and feet.

His human's expression held a mixture of confusion and disbelief when he returned his attention to Maelgwn. "Um, are you ... wanting me to join in cosplay or something?"

Tasker racked his brain on that one.

Cosplay? What's that?

25

Fortunately, Grigoris seemed just as confused, and he voiced the question. "What's cosplay?"

Aaden answered. "That's where people dress up as a fairy or wizard or knight or something, join up with a bunch of other like-minded people, and they carry out missions and role-play together." Shaking his head, Aaden told Camry, "No, this is not cosplay. This is real life." He pointed at Maelgwn. "He's really a gargoyle, although he's in his human form right now. We wanted to tell you about the paranormal before showing you," Aaden explained matter of factly. "That way, it wouldn't shock the hell out of you."

Camry clutched the handle of the duffle bag he carried over one shoulder in a near white-knuckled grip. "Um, why are you claiming this?" He quickly followed that up with, "And how could a gargoyle have a human skin? That doesn't make any sense from any of the stories I've read about them."

"What have you read about gargoyles?" Tobias asked, striding into the room. The second was in his human skin, just as the others were. "I'm curious about what's available out there."

"Well, originally, they were guardians. Uh, protectors. That's why they're on so many churches and cathedrals." Camry shrugged as he added, "And they're these grotesque winged beasts with fangs and claws and stuff." He scoffed softly, adding, "They certainly never turned into humans."

"Well, damn," Tasker muttered, unable to keep silent. Turning his head just enough to where he knew his features were in profile, he peered at Camry from the corner of his eye. "I would never have considered myself grotesque."

Camry's eyes widened in shock. "Oh my god." Then his eyes rolled to the back of his head, and he began to drop.

Tobias jumped forward and caught him, swinging him into his arms.

At the same time, Aaden snorted and said, "This is exactly

what we were trying to avoid, Tasker."

Chagrined, Tasker hunched his shoulders in embarrass-ment as he watched Tobias carry Camry to one of the sofas. Then, unable to help his instincts, he hurried to his mate's side. Tasker had just enough presence of mind to sit in a nearby chair rather than at the man's hip.

Tasker hated to admit it, but he didn't think Camry would appreciate waking up to him looming over him, holding his hand, no matter how much Tasker wished it to be.

CHAPTER FOUR

As Camry roused, he shifted, rubbing his head against the fabric beneath him. The sheets were cool against his cheek, and the mattress felt so much better than his own lumpy thing. He couldn't place where he was, as he didn't have any friends he would spend the night with.

Then it all came rushing back — the supposed dancing gig, paranormals, and gargoyles.

Camry snapped his eyes open to discover that he lay on a sofa — an extremely comfortable leather sofa. Mitch and Aaden sat on a sofa across from him, a coffee table between them. The guys that appeared to be their partners stood behind them, their hands resting proprietarily on their shoulders. The man who'd introduced himself as Maelgwn sat in a chair to the left with the man who'd entered a moment before Camry's freak-out standing nearby with his shoulder leaning against the wall.

Finally, sitting to Camry's other side . . . was the gargoyle.

Except, Camry had never seen a picture of a gargoyle that looked like this one. While the creature did indeed have wings, fangs, and claws, he was also extremely humanoid-looking. He was obviously bipedal with muscular limbs. His brow ridges were a little more pronounced, making them appear as eyebrows. His only hair appeared to be on his head, and that was white, like his wings and claws.

The biggest difference was the mottled-looking hide . . . which was a light blue.

"Oh god," Camry whispered, unable to tear his gaze from

28

the . . . gargoyle. "You're real."

The male—and it was obviously a male, with a fit body and six-pack abdominals—nodded his head. "I'm real. Gargoyles are real." His smile appeared a little uncertain when he curved up his full blue lips. "My name's Tasker. And I'm—"

"Let's wait on that reveal just yet, Tasker," Maelgwn cut in, stopping the male from saying whatever he'd intended. "So, I'm certain you have questions." He leaned forward, resting his forearms on his thighs. "Let's start with, would you like anything to eat or drink?" Maelgwn pointed at a nearby wall and the bar there. "It's fully stocked."

Do I want a drink?

Something alcoholic sounded pretty good right about then. Except, just like while he was at work, he figured he might need to keep his wits about him. That meant playing it safe.

"Um, a-a bottle of water, please," Camry requested.

Maelgwn smiled while the guy near him began to move.

"Playing it safe," Maelgwn commented, obviously knowing exactly what he'd been thinking. "Not a bad idea, under the circumstances." He turned his attention to the man who was now behind the bar. "I'll have a whiskey, Tobias."

Tobias nodded. "You got it, Chieftain." Then he smirked. "As if you even had to ask, after all these years."

Maelgwn chuckled as he turned his attention to those on the sofa. "We didn't really introduce everyone." He pointed toward the opposite sofa. "You know Mitch. The man behind him is Kardamon, his mate and also a gargoyle. And Aaden's partner is Grigoris. And, yes, a gargoyle, as am I and Tobias." Then Maelgwn pointed at Tasker. "Just as Tasker is."

Camry nodded slowly, glancing around at everyone. He noticed everyone else had left the room, probably while he slept. As Camry took the bottle of water from Tobias, he stared into the man's lightly bronzed features, trying to see any hint of anything . . . gargoyleish. He didn't see it.

Tobias smirked, but he didn't comment. Instead, he

handed off one of the tumblers he'd been carrying to Mael-gwn, keeping a second one for himself.

"I can't believe this is happening," Camry blurted out as he twisted the cap off the bottle, pleased to find that it was sealed. Then he took a deep swallow of his drink, enjoying the way the chill of the water cooled his throat.

"I was lucky," Mitch claimed. "I learned about these guys with Aziel and Andre, so we sort of had a support system with each other." With a laugh, he admitted, "We didn't have to freak out alone."

"I suppose I was lucky, too," Aaden spoke next. "When I found out, these guys already knew" — he used his thumb to indicate Mitch — "and they helped me through the freak-out." Tipping his chin up, Aaden peered at Grigoris behind him. "It helped that my mate was pushing for us to be together, and he was extremely persistent."

"You are worth it, my mate," Grigoris rumbled before bending at the waist and capturing Aaden's mouth in a deep, claiming kiss.

Maelgwn chuckled. Turning his attention to Tobias, he murmured, "Makes me want Bobby in the room."

Before he could stop himself, Camry asked, "Who's Bobby?"

"My own mate," Maelgwn told him, a sweet smile curving his lips, his love for the man on display for all to see. "He's in the playroom with our son and a few others with their young ones."

"You have a son?" Camry once again spoke without think-ing. Evidently, finding out gargoyles existed had broken his brain-to-mouth filter. Waving his hand, Camry quickly shook his head. "Um, sorry. This is really none of my business."

"It will be," Tasker murmured, his gaze intense upon Camry.

Camry had seen that type of hunger in the eyes of plenty

of men and women over the past several months. The gargoyle wanted him . . . sexually. He did his best to ignore his own burgeoning desire, thinking it was completely inappropriate.

Instead, Camry cleared his throat and returned his attention to Maelgwn, since he seemed to be the one who could give him the best answers. "Um, so . . . what am I doing here?" He glanced at Mitch for an instant before asking, "Why did I get invited here? Why would you tell me all this?"

Surely it was a secret, right?

Camry had certainly never heard one whisper about how these beings were more than just myth and legend.

"Well, you see," Maelgwn began, obviously choosing his words carefully. "Most paranormals live a lot longer than a human, which can lead to a very lonely existence. To counter that, Fate grants us a mate. Someone who completes us, in a way, as that person is the other half of our soul." Smiling, Maelgwn pointed at the couples across from him. "That's what these guys mean when they call each other mate. It's not just a term of endearment. It's a . . . connection."

Even as Camry nodded, he didn't think that answered his question at all. "O-Okay."

"Paranormals search for that special someone." Kardamon picked up the explanation. "And it doesn't matter if we find that person in a man, woman, human, or another paranormal species, we recognize them by scent, and we crave them above all others." The hand he had on Mitch's shoulder rubbed against him, seeming to pet him. "Our instinct is not just to care for the other half of our soul, but to please them and keep them safe, too. It's . . . almost a physical ache when we're kept apart for too long."

"Um, so . . . you gargoyles have a soul mate, and a human form, and you live here together in a"—Camry racked his brain for a second, trying to recall the word Maelgwn had used—"a clutch." That was it. "Um, what does this have to do with me, again?"

While Camry found the information dump interesting, he still didn't understand why they would invite him here.

Mitch chuckled, shaking his head. "Ya'll are taking the scenic route." Pointing at Tasker, he told him, "We snuck Tasker into the strip club Friday night. He scented you. You're his mate. The other half of his soul." As Camry's jaw sagged open, shock filling him, Mitch added, "So, that's why I convinced you to come here. So he'd have a safe place to meet you, and for you two to get to know each other." Mitch waggled his brows, and his insinuation was more than clear.

"Only when you're ready," Tasker quickly claimed. Resting his forearm on the arm of the chair closer to Camry, he assured, "We don't have to bond right away or anything. I know this is a lot to take in." Then he grimaced. His blue brow ridges furrowing as he muttered, "Of course, don't take that to mean I don't want you. I do. I really, *really* do. I just don't want you to feel pressured. I mean, working in a place like that, you must feel pressured to—"

During Tasker's verbal diarrhea, Tobias had moved. He clamped his hand over Tasker's mouth, ceasing his ramblings. With a sigh, he rubbed Tasker's shoulder soothingly.

Smiling at Camry, Tobias stated, "We can get a little excitable when we meet our mate."

Rubbing his forehead, Camry stared at the floor for a few seconds. He tried to process everything he'd just been told. There was a lot, and he wasn't totally certain where to begin.

Paranormals. Gargoyles. Mates. They think I am one.

The strip club.

Camry cocked his head, casting a side-eyed glance Tasker's way. The male was good-looking, in his own way. He wouldn't lie to himself and say he didn't find him attractive.

Deciding to start at the beginning, Camry mused, "So they snuck you into the strip club, and you somehow smelled me amidst all those people." He recalled Maelgwn saying they recognized their mate by scent. "How is that possible?"

Maelgwn answered. "While most paranormals have a much better sense of smell than a human, gargoyles surpass even them." He flicked out his tongue, revealing an appendage that appeared longer and narrower than any Camry had ever seen. Maelgwn continued to explain. "A gargoyle has sensory receptors on our tongue, not just in our nostrils. We can read the air currents in a room, which allows most of us to be excellent trackers."

Accepting that, as weird as Camry found it, he asked, "Why'd you have to sneak him in?" He focused on Mitch. "Why didn't he just change into his human form like the others?"

Tobias had returned to leaning against the wall where he explained, "A gargoyle doesn't have a human form until they bond with their mate."

Camry opened his mouth, then closed it again. He just didn't know what else to ask without sounding ignorant. Then he realized, he was indeed ignorant. He never would have suspected any of this.

"This is a lot to take in," Maelgwn rumbled kindly. "We understand that it is." Indicating Tasker, he explained, "Most paranormals dream of the day they find their mate. Tasker is the same. He just wants the opportunity to get to know you, to learn about you." Maelgwn grinned while chuckling softly. "Tasker's a good man, although he can be a bit impetuous at times."

"Like wanting to be snuck into the strip club," Aaden said, teasing in his tone. His dark eyes twinkled as he eyed Tasker. "Getting him out was harder than getting him in."

Tasker muttered, "I didn't want to leave Camry, especially with that asshole trying to paw at him."

"Yeah." Mitch jumped in. "Why'd you go sit with him after your last set? I thought you said he gave you the creeps."

Realizing they must have stuck around to watch him most of the evening, Camry felt an embarrassed flush rise up his neck. At times like this, he sure appreciated his dark complexion. After that disastrous date, Camry had stopped hanging out with people who knew what he did for a living.

Well, I don't hang out with people at all, really. No time.

"He does give me the creeps," Camry admitted, cringing as he recalled the feel of the man's hand on his thigh . . . way too far up his thigh due to the short-shorts he was forced to wear. "His name is Morgan Clarence, and he's rich, and I was there on my boss's orders."

"Dick," Mitch grumbled, scowling.

After that experience, Camry had begun worrying a little bit about what else his boss would order him to do in the name of *keeping the clients happy.*

"Shall I text Vane to look into him?" Tobias asked.

Maelgwn nodded.

Camry didn't know who that was, but Tobias seemed to be doing just that as he pulled his phone from his pocket and began tapping on the screen.

Falling silent, Camry couldn't help glancing toward Tasker a few times. Quiet filled the room. Shifting restlessly, Camry took another sip of his water.

"Okay, then," Maelgwn began, almost making Camry start. "Are you comfortable sitting and talking with Tasker, Camry?"

Am I?

Camry opened his mouth, then closed it again. A spike of anxiety surged through him, and it took every bit of self-control to keep from crunching his nearly empty bottle of water. After a second, he murmured, "A-Alone?"

After all, Camry knew that Tasker wanted him. He wasn't sure he believed the story about the whole mate thing. What if the gargoyle had seen him on the stage and decided he wanted him, and this was all an elaborate ruse put on by his friends to help him get the stripper into bed?

"If you want a chaperone, one of us can stay," Maelgwn assured. "Or all of us."

Camry watched Tasker's features turn almost stricken.

"You don't trust me," Tasker whispered. "You're afraid."

Having thought he had been doing a pretty good job of keeping his features straight, Camry blurted, "How could you tell?"

Maelgwn sighed and flicked his tongue out again. "Scent, Camry," he reminded him. "Our sense of smell is so well developed, we can read another person's emotions from the scents they put off." With a small smile, Maelgwn added, "We don't normally call attention to it unless it's important or necessary, but Tasker is correct. You've been pretty anxious all evening, which is completely understandable considering the big paranormal reveal." The big male waved his hand in a circle, as if to encompass everyone. "But the second we offered to give you a little privacy, that anxiety spiked into fear. So . . . want to tell us why?"

Camry clenched his jaw and breathed through his nose, taking one slow breath, then another. He tried to marshal his thoughts, but they were swirling inside his head. Black spots began to form across his vision.

"Okay, breathe, man." Mitch's hazy form bounced from his seat across from him, and he bounded over the coffee table. A second later, Mitch gripped the back of Camry's neck and forced his head between his knees. "Get your ass over here and trill, Tasker."

A second later, Camry felt a pair of strong arms wrap around him, wrapping his torso in a loose hold. That was followed up by something white.

Camry would have asked what it was if he could have even gotten enough air into his lungs.

Then . . . something happened. A strange vibrating noise

came from the gargoyle holding him. It seemed to seep into his body, then into his bones, and it even felt as if it warmed him from the inside out.

Suddenly, Camry could breathe again.

"Oh, wow," Camry whispered. "What's that?"

CHAPTER FIVE

Relief filled Tasker as he felt Camry's stiff body begin to relax against him. Continuing to trill, he rubbed one palm up and down his mate's back soothingly. He rested his other palm on his human's opposite hip, teasing his thumb over his hip bone.

A little too prominent, in my opinion.

Tasker felt a surge of need to care for Camry. He'd seen where the man was living. He'd run across him while he was working. According to Raymond's information, Camry had no communication with family, and he had no social media accounts.

Camry didn't even have a credit card.

My mate needs someone in his corner, and I plan to be that someone . . . if I can convince him.

Unable to help himself, Tasker rested his cheek against Camry's bleached-blond hair. The short, wiry strands were a little rough against his flesh. He enjoyed the sensation as he rubbed his cheek back and forth, continuing to trill and soothe his human.

Upon hearing Camry's quiet exclamation and soft question, Tasker smiled. He didn't stop his ministrations even as he answered. "This is called trilling," Tasker explained. "It's an ability unique to a gargoyle." Keeping his voice as soothing as possible, he added, "Gargoyles are unique in the paranormal world. We don't get a human form until after we've found our soul mate and completed our bond with him or her.

Sometimes, a human can get overwhelmed by the sudden expansion of their world, so Fate gave us this ability to soothe them." After placing a kiss to Camry's dark temple, Tasker added, "We also use it to relax sick or injured family, friends, or younglings."

"Huh."

"It's a really cool sensation to feel during sex, too," Mitch stated with a husky chuckle.

The human had returned to his seat, for which Tasker was grateful, even with the human's timely intervention. Still, he wanted to smack the man upside the head at times for his big mouth. As soon as Mitch's comment seemed to register with Camry, Tasker felt his mate tense.

Evidently, sex was a sensitive subject for Camry. While Tasker found that odd, considering his line of work, he didn't question it. Instead, he just kept trilling until Camry relaxed once more.

When Camry lifted his head, to Tasker's pleasure, he didn't attempt to pull away from him. In fact, he seemed to press his shoulder harder into Tasker's chest. He sighed deeply as he glanced around the room.

Maelgwn and Tobias were talking quietly between themselves. Mitch and Kardamon were watching Tasker, perhaps to make certain all went well with Camry. Aaden and Grigoris had moved to the bar and were currently pouring drinks.

"Um, sorry to, uh . . . freak out, I guess."

Camry's muttered words seemed to draw everyone's attention, and if Tasker didn't miss his guess, he would bet that if Camry's skin wasn't so dark, he would be sporting a flush.

Hopefully, soon I'll be able to make his skin heat for a different reason.

Tasker's eager dick gave a twitch at his thoughts, and he quickly shut down that line of thinking. When his mate had started hyperventilating, he'd softened, even while holding his mate. Upon feeling his tension at the mention of sex, Tasker needed to keep his arousal in check.

Gods, I hope my mate wasn't abused.

While Tasker figured it was a myth, he'd heard somewhere that many strippers went into that line of work because of some abuse in their past somewhere.

"No need to apologize, Camry," Maelgwn offered, returning his attention to them. "If you hadn't freaked out, it would have been more surprising." His smile appeared kind as he continued, "These are shocking revelations. We know that."

"Ready for a different drink, Camry?" Grigoris called from the bar. "Or another bottle of water? We have juice and soda back here, too."

"Um, I-I'm not sure. Some fireball whiskey would be fantastic," Camry admitted. Then his brows furrowed. "But I'm a lightweight, so I really shouldn't be drinking. I still have to drive home later."

Upon hearing Camry mentioning leaving, Tasker couldn't help but tighten his arms just a little. He did manage to keep in his growl of displeasure. Tasker grimaced, forcing back the words to counter the idea of his mate's leaving.

I can't force him to stay. He's human. I have to woo him.

"Why don't you stay the night," Aaden offered, bringing a glass containing an amber liquid toward the sofa. Grinning, he waved the hand toward Camry enticingly, and Tasker's sensitive nose picked up the scent of the cinnamon-flavored whiskey. "There are plenty of spare bedrooms in the estate," he told him. "Just like we said. You're perfectly safe here, and no one will expect more from you than you're willing to give."

After a few seconds of hesitation, Camry began reaching for the glass, and Tasker eased his wings from around his mate so he could take it. "I-If you're s-sure?" He glanced around the group, his gaze flicking between Maelgwn and Tasker and back again.

Maelgwn nodded once. "I know Tasker is holding you right now, and he didn't really ask permission to do that, but it was to help you calm down." He pointed at the pair. "If you were to ask him to remove his arms from you, he would." Then he smiled sadly. "Although he would be deeply disappointed."

"I, uh . . . I don't mind so much," Camry murmured, sounding so damn shy. He even peered at Tasker through his lashes.

It was such a sweet look, and Tasker wondered what it would be like to debauch his mate. His lips were just begging to be kissed, and he wanted to lick every inch of the muscled body he'd seen twisting around the pole Friday evening. His palms itched to cradle Camry's firm ass as he plunged inside his hot depths, taking them to the heights of ecstasy.

Predictably, his body responded to the images filling his head, forcing him to turn his focus to something else.

My mate freaked out just at the idea of being alone with me. Remember that.

Tasker did his best to bank his desire, which helped keep his smile free of his heated thoughts. "I'm glad to hear that." Releasing Camry's hip with the hand wrapped around his stomach, he replaced it with the palm that had been stroking his spine. With his newly freed hand, Tasker lightly touched Camry's jaw while admitting, "I like holding you."

Camry didn't respond. Instead, he took a sip of the whiskey, probably trying to hide his embarrassment. His scent gave him away, however.

"So, are you ready to ask us questions?" Maelgwn asked, returning to his seat, a fresh tumbler in hand.

"It was nice to meet you," Tobias cut in, heading toward the door. "I have a few other things to catch up on before I can meet up with Roland." With a smirk, the second added, "I just stopped by because I wanted to meet Tasker's mate."

Then the gargoyle exited the room, closing the door behind

him.

"So, um . . . you say you're all gargoyles," Camry began, glancing at the big men. "It's hard to believe." He cradled his drink in both hands, but his nerves had him tapping the glass. "Can you prove it?"

"Sure we can," Maelgwn replied. His smile appeared kind as he asked, "Are you certain you're ready to see more of our kind?"

"Well, according to you, I'm already looking at them," Camry said.

"You just can't tell," Grigoris reminded him. "We don't want to scare or upset you."

"I want to see what you mean when you say human skin," Camry insisted.

Maelgwn nodded. "One at a time, then. So we don't over-whelm you." Then he nodded at Grigoris.

Grigoris pulled his shirt from over his head and draped it over the back of the sofa near Aaden's head.

Camry tensed within the cradle of Tasker's arms. "Why's he undressing?"

Before Tasker could answer, Grigoris did. "Because I don't want to ruin my shirt," he explained. Pointing at Tasker, he stated, "I have wings, too."

A second later, Camry's jaw sagged open as he watched Grigoris change. The male's six-foot-three body grew several inches, and his shoulders became even broader. His light brown skin darkened to a deep mottled gray. Black claws replaced his fingernails, and Tasker knew the same would be on his toes. Finally, huge black wings appeared behind him, having grown from his shoulder blades.

Those in the room seemed to hold their collective breaths as they waited for Camry's response.

After a few heartbeats, Camry let out a noise that sounded suspiciously like an *eep*, but that was it.

Finally, Maelgwn asked, "Are you certain you would like us to continue, Camry?"

Camry took what was probably a fortifying gulp of his drink. While his dark eyes were wide, he still nodded.

Kardamon followed next, revealing his slightly smaller but still impressive medium-blue hide and white wings. After that, Maelgwn rose from his chair, pulled his shirt from him and kicked off his shoes, and did the same. His chieftain sported a dark-blue hide and black wings and claws.

Glancing around at them all, Camry continued to gape. They allowed him to stare for several minutes. Finally, Tasker couldn't help but reach over and gently touch his forefingers under the man's chin, urging him to close his mouth.

Snapping his attention to Tasker, Camry whispered, "So, after you bond, you'll be able to change into a human form, too?"

"I will," Tasker confirmed. While he worried that Camry didn't appreciate his gargoyle body, he kept that concern to himself. He took a few seconds to explain molt to his mate. "Then I'll be able to roost whenever I wish, and I'll be able to remain awake during daylight hours, so I can spend more time with you."

"Oh, so non-bonded gargoyles sleep as stone statues during the day?" Camry cocked his head. "That's true?"

"That's true," Maelgwn confirmed.

Camry glanced around the group, then asked, "Do gargoyles ever lie about who their mate is, so they can bond, just so they can go through molt and no longer have to sleep as a statue every day?"

Tasker's mate had said the words so swiftly that it took him a second to figure out what his human had said. When he did, he sucked in a shocked breath. The other gargoyles responded with narrowed eyes, and Maelgwn growled softly.

Wincing, perhaps realizing he'd said something wrong,

Camry hunched his shoulders and ducked his head.

"No," Maelgwn replied softly, yet firmly. "No gargoyle would ever do that. A fate-given mate is sacrosanct. A gift from the gods." A quiet growl rumbled within his voice as he continued, "Any paranormal who would try such a thing would instantly be labeled rogue and turned over to the elders. We never lie when it comes to Fate's gifts."

"Besides," Grigoris cut in roughly. "Paranormals can tell when another is lying, so it would be foolish to try anyway."

Rubbing Camry's back, Tasker did his best to soothe his still-tense human. He thought about trilling again. He'd just decided to do just that when Camry relaxed in his hold.

"Sorry," Camry whispered again. "I didn't mean any offense."

Maelgwn heaved a deep sigh. Then he relaxed in his chair, as if that action alone had released all his tension. "You didn't know," he stated. "How are you to learn if you don't ask?"

"So, you think I'm your mate," Camry mused, peering at Tasker.

Even though it wasn't a question, Tasker still replied, "Yes, Camry. You are most definitely my mate." Then he smiled and added, "That means I'm your mate, too, and I'll do my damnedest to make your life better in every way possible."

Camry continued to eye him for a moment before he slowly nodded once.

Tasker felt as if he'd just won the lottery. He felt certain his mate had just agreed to be his. His human's next question proved that it wasn't quite that simple or easy.

Turning his attention on Mitch and Aaden, Camry stated, "I get what's in it for them." He waggled his finger between the gargoyles as he took a sip of his whiskey. Once he'd swallowed, Camry continued, "I'm getting that this bonding thing is like marriage." Once Aaden had nodded in confirmation,

Camry asked, "What's in it for you guys? I mean, as the humans? You're both . . . what? Early twenties? How can you think you're ready to settle down with one guy at that age?"

To Tasker's surprise, both men chuckled as they exchanged a look. Neither appeared offended or concerned by the question.

Aaden arched a black brow. "Do you want to go first?"

Shaking his head, Mitch waved a hand. "Naw. Fire away."

"I was deep in the closet when I met Grigoris. Just trying to finish college so I could move away and get away from my family," Aaden admitted. "And my family were part of this group that hunts gargoyles, not that I knew it at the time." Shrugging, Aaden admitted, "Finding a permanent love interest wasn't even a blip on my radar, so I understand the question. But" — he turned a warm gaze on Grigoris — "giving Grigoris a chance was the best damn decision I ever made." Aaden returned his focus to Camry. "You see, when a gargoyle says they want to care for you and make you happy in all ways, they mean it." Scoffing, he added, "And that's not just the sex. I'm talking in *all* ways. They support you in your dreams and encourage you every step of the way." Reaching up, Aaden rested his hand over Grigoris's, who had returned it to Aaden's shoulder after he'd returned to his true form. "I look forward to every day I get to wake up with this gargoyle, and feel grateful for every evening I lie down beside him. He's the best thing that could ever have happened to me."

"Thank you, my mate," Grigoris rumbled thickly. He blinked quickly a few times before rounding the sofa and grabbing Aaden into his arms. In the next instant, Grigoris fused his mouth to Aaden's as he moved to a stool on the other side of the room. When Grigoris broke the kiss, they started whispering to each other.

Mitch chuckled, drawing everyone's attention. "That was so sweet I feel like I should floss so I don't get a toothache."

Kardamon scoffed before bending at the waist and putting his mouth near Mitch's ear. "That wasn't what you were telling me when you were reaming my ass this morning."

"You bottom?" Camry blurted, obviously shocked at the idea of the large gargoyle allowing his much smaller human to top him.

Waggling his brows, Mitch nodded. "Yep, he bottoms." With a wry scoff, he continued, "Hell, I'm not gay for anyone but this guy." Mitch shook his head as he admitted, "I still think Kardamon got the short end of the stick when it comes to mates. What with all the hoops I made him jump through when we first got together."

"We made it work, Mitch," Kardamon cut in, wrapping his arms around Mitch from behind. "We're still making it work . . .every day."

Mitch turned his head and pressed a kiss to Kardamon's jaw. "Yeah, we do."

Tasker heard Camry take a shaky breath, and he wondered what his human would make of the pair's revelations.

CHAPTER SIX

Camry swallowed the last of his whiskey, the cinnamon-flavored alcohol warming him from the inside out.

Or maybe that's caused by the answer to my question.

While the pair hadn't said it outright, Camry caught it just the same. The two couples had come together to overcome their problems. They even still seemed to be working together toward . . . something.

The looks that passed between them told the story. They weren't just in love. The pairs showed a mutual respect and dedication to their relationship.

They have peace.

That was something Camry hadn't felt in so very long. He eyed Tasker in the peripheral of his vision for a few seconds. Could he have that with this gargoyle?

Peace with a gargoyle. What a novel idea.

"Did you know anything about each other when you got together?" Camry asked, peering at Mitch since Aaden was still sitting on the other side of the room.

Mitch shook his head, then squinted his eyes as he waggled his head back and forth a little.

What did that mean?

"I found out about gargoyles almost a year before I ran into Kardamon and he claimed I was his mate," Mitch told him. He nibbled his bottom lip for a second, then admitted, "So, I knew what he was telling me, and I understood my totally weird attraction to him." With a scoff, Mitch reminded him, "I'd never been with a guy before, so getting a hard-on for this one really wigged me out. I had some adjusting up here" — Mitch tapped the side of his head — "before I finally gave Kardamon a chance. It was worth it, though."

"Thank you again, my mate," Kardamon rumbled, kissing the side of Mitch's neck.

"So, no. I didn't know Kardamon, and he didn't know me," Mitch continued. "We had to get to know each other, and Kard did that by milking info about me from my friends, since I wouldn't talk to him." Mitch turned and pecked Kardamon's jaw again. "Thanks for being patient with me."

"Always, my mate," Kardamon rumbled back, a warmth filling his dark eyes. "Always."

Focusing on Tasker, Camry told him, "I don't have any friends for you to pump for information about me." Then he grimaced and admitted, "Well, all my old friends would warn you away because I'm a fag. Coming out was . . . a mistake."

"Being true to yourself is never a mistake," Tasker countered, his brow ridges furrowing. "But I'm sorry that your family and friends turned their back on you." Grimacing, he added, "One of our tech guys, Raymond, looked into you. He told me you didn't speak with your family, and now I know why."

Camry felt his cheeks heat as he shifted uncomfortably in his seat. "Um, yeah." Holding up his tumbler, he asked, "Can I get a bit more?"

"Sure," Kardamon instantly agreed, moving toward him. "As long as you agree you're not driving anywhere tonight."

Nodding once, Camry replied, "Agreed."

Kardamon plucked the tumbler from between his fingers with a nod and a smile.

As Camry waited for his drink, he asked, "So, how do you all date and get to know each other if you don't look human?" He cocked his head as he eyed Tasker speculatively. "How's that work?"

"If you want to go on dates," Tasker began slowly. "We can have a picnic in the gardens. Or take a moonlit walk out by the pond." Humming, Tasker seemed to be thinking quickly before he added, "A barbeque with my people, so I can introduce you to them, and they can tell you embarrassing stories about me."

"Just remember to remind our people not to talk about who you have and haven't had sex with," Kardamon reminded as he returned and handed Camry his drink. "We don't want to hear about our mate's past sexual exploits any further than it will take us to know what positions they enjoy and what to stay away from." Kardamon sat down next to Mitch and handed him a new beer. "And our people should offer you the same courtesy, Camry."

"Well, that's not hard," Camry muttered, deciding to take the plunge. Or maybe his brazenness was caused by the alcohol. "I've never had full-on sex before. Other than kissing a couple of guys and knowing I prefer the feel of a guy's hand on my dick more than a girl's, I couldn't tell you what I liked."

Tasker sucked in a harsh breath, drawing Camry's attention to his face. The way the gargoyle stared at him . . . as if famished and Camry was a twenty-four-ounce steak . . . caused a mixture of desire and embarrassment to surge through him. That time, as his face and dick filled with blood in equal measure, Camry didn't think even his dark complexion could completely hide his blush.

"Oh, my mate," Tasker rumbled, his fingers twitching where they rested on Camry's hip. "When the time comes, I will be honored with the gift you'll be granting me." Then his expression sobered, and he admitted, "I'm over four hundred years old. I've been around the block a time or twelve. There are those in the clutch that'll tell you I'm a slut, and they would be right."

The words Tasker admitted caused Camry's gut to twist

and bounce, as if it were suddenly filled with butterflies. The male before him was obviously experienced. Camry couldn't imagine how he could possibly please someone of Tasker's—

Wait.

"D-Did you just say you're over four *hundred* years old?" Camry's brain stalled on that. "How's that possible?"

Even though Camry didn't think that was what he should be focusing on, he couldn't seem to help himself.

Four hundred years?

Tasker nodded slowly. "We mentioned paranormals are long-lived," he reminded Camry. "Gargoyles are the longest-lived that are natural to this plane."

"This plane?" Camry waved his hand. "Never mind. We can talk about that another time when my mind isn't already blown." He took a deep gulp of his drink, feeling his head swim just a little. Touching his temple, Camry whispered, "Four hundred."

"Yes," Tasker confirmed. "Four-hundred-thirty-eight this coming summer, although I don't remember the exact date." He shrugged, his expression betraying that he saw this as no consequence. "Gargoyles can live upward of two thousand years, baring something unexpected."

"Then why the hell would you want to saddle yourself with a human?" Camry didn't get it. "I'll die in less than a hundred, and you'll be left alone again."

That didn't seem so fair on Fate's part.

"We seem to have left out a few bits," Maelgwn commented with a quiet scoff. "Sorry about that." With a wry smile, he explained, "When a gargoyle and his mate finish their bond, their life threads become linked. Intertwined, if you will. That person's life will extend to match the gargoyle's."

Oh. Camry's mouth formed the word, but no sound came out.

"We've left out a lot of bits," Mitch cut in. "But there

doesn't seem to be any help for it. There's just so much to explain." He shrugged. "We'll get it all out there eventually." With a wink, Mitch added, "Just remember to eat something with cinnamon in it every day. Trust me. We'll explain after you've processed what we've already told you."

"Okay," Camry whispered, because what else could he say?

Camry rubbed at his temple, his eyelids growing heavy. While he was used to working late into the night, this was a little different. Camry didn't ever drink while doing that. Plus, he was either doing something strenuous that kept his blood pumping, or he was busy being paranoid about where the next inappropriate touch would come from.

"I think it's time for you to show Camry to his room," Maelgwn stated, rising from his seat. He glanced at his phone once, then told him, "It's right across the hall from your own. Sumak volunteered to set it up for you." Even on his deep blue gargoyle face, Maelgwn's expression appeared kind. "You'll find sweatpants and other necessities in the dresser and bathroom. Please, feel free to use whatever you like."

After Tasker helped Camry to his feet — *wow, when did I get so tired* — Maelgwn held out his hand to him. "I know it's a little premature," he began, pausing until Camry placed his hand in the huge male's, surprised to find the hold gentle. "But I'd like to be the first to welcome you to my clutch. Tasker is a good man, and I hope you'll give him the chance to prove that to you."

Nodding once more, Camry felt as if his tongue was tied. These gargoyles had offered him more kindness than his own family. After months on his own, barely scraping by and having to constantly watch his own back, he didn't know how to respond to that.

"I'll show you the way," Tasker told him.

When Camry turned to face him, he realized the male

wasn't any taller than himself . . . and he already had Camry's duffel bag strap over his shoulder.

"O-Okay."

Camry downed the last of his whiskey, and before he could decide where to put the tumbler, Kardamon took it from his fingers. "Get some rest," the big male urged. "Text Mitch when you wake, and we'll come collect you. We'll give you a tour of the estate."

Once again, Camry could just nod.

After getting good-byes from the pair across the room, Camry followed Tasker out of the large recreation room.

Tasker smiled at him and asked, "May I hold your hand?"

After a few seconds of hesitation, Camry nodded. He took the gargoyle's blue hand in his own. The feel of the callouses on his fingers as he wrapped them around Camry's digits caused the hairs on his arm to stand on end, and goose bumps erupted up his limb.

Oh, wow. What will those feel like on my dick?

Having difficulty controlling himself—it had been so long since he'd felt lust—Camry tried to ignore the way his blood flowed south and the way his dick was plumping in his jeans. At least he was wearing one of his relaxed-fit jeans, so he had more room. He'd intended to change into something more provocative to dance, after all.

That was when it hit Camry that, in his tired state, he hadn't thought twice about being alone with his escort. Maybe that was because he'd been nothing but kind and, well, sweet. He'd also been earnest and straightforward, being honest about what some might consider his own shortcomings.

I have a lot to think about.

Tasker led Camry down the hall, up two flights of stairs, and along another hall. The gargoyle was smiling as he stated, "I know it can be a bit confusing at first, but I'm sure you'll get the hang of it soon enough."

"Uh, okay." Camry nibbled his bottom lip, realizing quickly what the man's words meant.

Tasker intended for him to spend plenty of time at the estate . . . enough to learn the layout.

And tomorrow, Kardamon and Mitch will be giving me a tour. What did it all mean?

Needing sleep to process everything, Camry did his best to stop thinking about it. The answers would come in time.

Tasker stopped at a door and opened it for him. Then he pointed at the one across the hall. "If you need anything, I'll be right in there until sunrise."

"Where will you be after that?" Camry asked without thinking as he moved into the room. "Oh, wow."

The suite was finer than any hotel he'd ever been in. There was a large front sitting area with a lounge recliner and a big TV on the wall. There was a nook with a coffee maker and mini-fridge. Through the arch in the back, Camry spotted the corner of a bed. An open door in that direction revealed a bit of a bathroom counter.

"I hope you'll be comfortable," Tasker murmured. With a squeeze of Camry's hand, reminding him that the gargoyle held it, Tasker drew his attention. "And I'll be up there." He pointed straight up. "Roosting on the roof."

Recalling what he'd asked, Camry felt his eyes widen. "Oh, right."

How silly of me.

Tasker lifted their twined fingers to his mouth. Holding Camry's gaze, he gently kissed Camry's knuckle. Then he whispered, "I hope you sleep well, Camry. I'll see you soon."

Camry nodded dumbly, his mind thoroughly blown.

After Tasker kissed his knuckle again, even though his heated gaze lingered on Camry's lips through it all, the gargoyle released him and strode from the room. He paused in the hall and turned around to face him.

"Will you do me a favor and lock the door behind me,

please?"

Before Camry could question the order—he was supposed to be safe, according to the chieftain, after all—Tasker quickly added, "I know it's an irrational request, but I can't seem to help myself. Just . . . please?"

Hearing the soft plea in Tasker's voice, Camry knew he couldn't refuse. Besides, he'd intended to lock his door anyway—habit, after all.

Camry crossed to the door and slowly began swinging it shut. Just before it closed, he spotted Tasker's look of longing, and he couldn't resist. Opening it a little wider, Camry beckoned.

Arching one brow ridge, Tasker obeyed.

Leaning forward, Camry pressed a chaste kiss to Tasker's lips. He heard the male's gasp, then his moan. But Camry's courage broke, and he hurriedly separated their lips and shut the door, barely catching himself before he slammed it. Camry locked it, then turned to face the room.

"Wow," he muttered again, but for a whole new reason. "I just kissed a gargoyle . . . and I really want to do it again."

After a shake of his head and a glance toward the door behind him, Camry headed deeper into the room to explore.

An epic hot shower with amazing water pressure later, Camry pulled on a pair of sleep shorts and climbed under the covers. His body sank into the mattress, and he felt as if he were being cradled in a cloud. As Camry fell asleep, he feared he would be ruined forever by experiencing just this one night at the gargoyle estate.

CHAPTER SEVEN

Tasker felt the knife sink into the flesh of his forefinger, and he hissed, more from being startled than from being in pain. He dropped the knife and quickly moved his bleeding hand away from the pile of potatoes he was dicing. Grabbing a hand towel, Tasker quickly wrapped it around his injured digit.

"You okay?" Kort asked, stopping beside the counter beside him. He glanced from the potatoes to Tasker and back again. "What happened?"

"Knife just slipped," Tasker claimed, watching Kort move the knife, which still had traces of his blood on it, to the dirty dishes sink.

"Yeah, right." Kort smirked at him. The deep red gargoyle was the second in command of the kitchens and had the right to boot Tasker out if he didn't get his act together.

"I'll be more careful," Tasker promised. Due to his increased gargoyle healing, he would bet his finger was already healed beneath the towel, but he hesitated to remove it until Kort moved on.

"Heard you found your mate," Kort commented, sounding way too casual. He glanced at him side-eyed. "Where and when? Human?"

Kort knew he couldn't lie, and he would never deny his mate, anyway. "I did." Thinking of Camry, he couldn't help but smile. "He's gorgeous. Toned from dancing, and bendy." Sighing deeply, he recalled some of his mate's moves, wondering how long it would take before he could put his mate's flexibility to use in bed. "So bendy," Tasker whispered.

"You're such a horndog," Twilden cut in with a sneer. "You want your mate for one thing. Sex." Glaring at Tasker, the small yellow gargoyle asked, "You gonna compare his dick to Beldrew's, too? Maybe I should warn him that your brain-to-mouth filter is shit in bed. He—"

"Twilden, that's enough," Kort snapped harshly. His blue eyes flashed with clear warning as he snarled, "You know the law. Coming between fated mates is taboo."

Twilden crossed his arms over his lean torso and jutted his chin out belligerently. "How do we know this human is really Tasker's fated mate?" His eyes narrowed as he mused, "He spotted him at that strip club. Maybe he's just horny since me and Beldrew have refused to touch him. I'd be doing this guy a favor by—"

"Chieftain Maelgwn and Second Tobias have already met with Tasker and his human," Kort snarled, revealing he knew plenty more than what he'd been letting on to Tasker. "Do you honestly think they would allow that kind of subterfuge to continue if Tasker wasn't telling the truth?" Without waiting for Twilden to reply, Kort ordered, "You have dishwashing duty for the next week. I'll make the necessary scheduling changes shortly." Pointing at the pile of dishes still needing to be done, the chef stated, "Better get started."

Gasping in clear outrage, Twilden stared in disbelief for all of two seconds. When Kort didn't change his command, the small gargoyle growled under his breath as he spun away from them. He flounced across the room, giving away his anger even more than the spicy scent emanating from him.

As soon as Twilden started the water running, Tasker muttered, "He has a right to be upset with me." He winced as he began pulling off the towel, and not because there was any pain, since there wasn't any. His wound had healed. "I really put my foot in it with him."

"No one deserves to have threats made against their fated mate, Tasker," Kort rumbled, patting him on the back. "I'll be reporting his comment to Enforcer Einan," he told him, referring to their clutch's head enforcer. "He'll need to be watched, just in case he decides to do something stupid in his anger."

Tasker grimaced. "Shit. I don't want him in trouble."

"That's because you're a good guy." Smirking, Kort added, "A little thoughtless in bed, so watch yourself with your mate, but good, nonetheless." Then he started sliding the potato chunks that had drops of Tasker's blood on them into his palm. "Also, you shouldn't be wielding a knife when you're so distracted." Kort offered him a commiserating smile as he tidied up Tasker's mess. "Go do laundry, instead."

Nodding, Tasker offered, "Thanks. I appreciate it."

Then Tasker headed to the laundry room, the bloodied towel still in his hand.

"Will you come to the estate after your shift?" Tasker did his best to keep his desperation out of his tone, but he certainly felt that way—desperate. He hadn't seen his mate in forty-eight hours, and already he felt as if he were about to go out of his mind with need.

While Tasker had met Camry at the strip club, he hadn't given it much thought on how that would impact their schedules. His mate worked well into the night. He'd worked Monday, but was supposed to have Tuesday evening off. Except, once again, his asshole boss had called him in.

That meant Camry would be working his third night in a row, and Tasker desperately wanted his mate to come to him after his shift.

"I normally just shower and crash after my shift," Camry hedged. "I wouldn't make very good company."

Good company or not, Tasker wanted him at the estate.

In fact —

"If you come here, I can massage your sore muscles after

your shower." Another idea struck Tasker. "Or, I have a jetted tub in my suite that's big enough for two. I could put some oil in the water and massage you in there." Hearing the silence coming from the other end of the line, Tasker winced.

Right. Virgin.

"Or I could just hold you, feed you chocolates and strawberries, and we could wear our shorts."

"Um, okay." Camry's quiet response finally came through the line. "I, uh, normally get off at two or thereabouts."

"I'll be waiting," Tasker assured.

Eagerly waiting.

"Well, I gotta go." Camry sounded reluctant, even though he'd already said that to Tasker once.

With Camry's promise to visit after work achieved, Tasker was willing to close the line. "Have a good shift, Camry. A safe shift," he murmured. "I look forward to seeing you."

"I, uh . . . me, too." Then Camry disconnected the line.

Clutching the phone to his chest, Tasker thought about his words.

Have a safe shift.

Without a human form, Tasker couldn't assure that outcome himself, but that didn't mean he couldn't do his best to make it happen.

Quickly dialing Enforcer Einan, Tasker tapped his forefinger on his thigh.

"Hello, Tasker," Einan greeted. "I was wondering if I'd hear from you."

"I, uh . . . really?"

He had been?

Einan chuckled, deep and soft. "Sure. Your mate is working at a strip club, and you can't be there." Tasker could hear the amusement in the man's voice. "You want someone to keep an eye on him for you."

"Uh, yes, sir," Tasker immediately replied. "I do."

"Already on it," Einan assured him. "Tible has never been

to a strip club, so he and Gus are going tonight," he told him, referring to a young gargoyle — well, by their standards, as he was less than a century old — and his shifter mate. Gus shared his spirit with a white rhino and was built like a bodybuilder. While both were actually gentle souls, Tasker knew they could handle any issue that came up.

Einan continued talking, pulling Tasker out of his thoughts.

"I'm passing the word around to see what mated couples might be interested," Einan told him. "It'll change every time, so keep me posted on his shifts."

"His boss has been calling him in a lot," Tasker admitted, growling in frustration. "There's a rich client he's trying to schmooze."

"Hmmm," Einan mused. "And that rich client likes your mate."

Although Einan didn't phrase it like a question, Tasker still growled, "Yup."

"Oh, that's the Morgan guy Maelgwn and Tobias were telling me about," Einan stated, revealing he understood the score. "I'll give everyone his picture. His boss, too." His tone turned hard. "I think we'll take a look into him as well. What's his name?"

"Uh, I don't know," Tasker admitted. "I know he's the owner, though."

"Okay. That'll be easy enough to figure out," Einan claimed. "If anything comes up, I'll contact you."

"Thank you, sir," Tasker quickly replied, barely getting the words out before Einan had closed the call.

Flopping back on the bed, Tasker stared at the ceiling. Relief that Camry was being monitored flooded him, causing tension he hadn't even realized he carried to melt from his shoulders.

My mate will be here before too long.

Tasker peered toward the bathroom.

Time to scrub the tub.

With that thought in mind and a grin on his face, Tasker bounced from the bed and settled in to clean his ensuite.

By two-fifteen, Tasker had begun to pace the front hall. He couldn't help it, even though he knew there was no way that Camry would arrive that swiftly. The strip club was nearly forty-five minutes away — thirty-five of those minutes on the other side of Durango.

Just as he turned to make another pass, Tasker's phone rang. He spotted Gus's name and quickly accepted the call. "Hey, Gus." Concern raced through his system, and his tension ratcheted back up. "Is everything okay?"

"It will be." Gus's deep voice came through the line. "I've got ya on speaker phone."

"Okay." Tasker frowned. "What's up?"

"Camry just needs assurances that me and Tible are on the up and up," Gus told him. "He's here with me."

"Camry? You there?" Tasker immediately called.

"Yeah, I'm here." Camry sounded a mixture of tired and upset with a side of uncertainty. "They said they were your friends, but you can never be too careful these days."

Tasker nodded, even though he knew his mate couldn't see it. "True enough. They live here at the estate with me."

"Oh, so they're . . ." Camry's voice trailed off, but his intent was clear enough.

"Yeah. Friends of mine," Tasker confirmed again. "What's wrong?"

Tasker couldn't recall getting a clear answer on that. Why would Camry need to know Gus was his friend unless . . ."What happened?"

"I have a flat tire," Camry admitted. "And my spare is flat, too." His frustration came through loud and clear. "They offered a ride, but I needed to make certain they weren't affiliated with—" Camry cut himself off and cleared his throat.

"Anyway, I'll get a ride with them and worry about my car tomorrow, I guess."

"Definitely catch a ride with them," Tasker encouraged, relieved that his mate wasn't alone in his problem. "But I know my people will be willing to take care of your car for you. We'll get it fixed."

"What? Why would you—" Camry began, sounding confused. "You don't have to—"

"Oh, baby," Tasker cut in softly. "You're not alone anymore. You have help." Filling his tone with encouragement, he ordered, "Get in Gus and Tible's truck and relax on the ride home, uh, here." He winced at the slip of the tongue, but it was too late to do anything about it. "I'll ask about who can head out to retrieve your car, and I'm sure it'll be waiting right here in the morning for you."

Tasker crossed his fingers, hoping he wasn't lying to his mate. Even unmated, surely his clutch mates would help.

"Thanks, Tasker." That time, Camry's voice was filled with relief.

"See you soon, baby," Tasker offered.

"Yeah."

Then Gus came back on. "Tible already called Einan," he revealed. "Grigoris is coming with a spare and a second person to drive Camry's car, but I'm still going to bring him to you." His voice lowered as he murmured, "He got hassled a bit by that rich asshole, and it looked like the bastard was going to come over here in the parking lot, but he took one look at me and took off." Then Gus added, "Your man could use a little pampering."

Tasker growled softly upon hearing that news, but he assured Gus, "I have pampering all set up."

"Good. See you soon."

Gus didn't wait for a response, and Tasker once again found himself calling Einan.

"I heard," Einan stated in lieu of a greeting. "Grigoris is taking a tire out there, and Sumak is going to drive Camry's sedan." With a scoff, the enforcer stated, "Hell, by the time Camry wakes up in the morning, I bet his car will be running better than it ever has."

Smiling, Tasker figured that was true. It was common knowledge that Grigoris loved tinkering on all kinds of vehicles. Any time a new mate joined their clutch, he would inspect their ride from top to bottom and fix even the tiniest of problems.

"Thank you for sending them out," Tasker still stated. "I appreciate it."

"Yup. Have a good night now."

When Einan hung up again, Tasker couldn't help but grin upon hearing the mirth—and even the hint of innuendo—in the enforcer's voice.

Yes. I certainly hope to have a good night.

Forty minutes later, Tasker spotted headlights coming up the driveway. He hurried to the garage and waited just inside the man-sized door. A garage bay door opened, and he watched Gus's huge truck roll into the cavernous space.

The driver's side door opened, but the passenger side did not.

As Tasker strode toward the vehicle, he watched both Gus and Tible slide out. He opened his mouth to question the rhino shifter, but the big man lifted a finger to his lips in the *be quiet* sign. His lips were curved into a smile, and his dark eyes twinkled with amusement.

Once Tasker reached the truck, Gus pointed at the passenger side window, and Tasker saw what seemed to be pleasing the man. Gus hadn't been kidding about Camry needing some TLC. Tasker's human sat with his head against the passenger side window. His eyes were closed, and he was fast asleep.

"My poor mate," Tasker murmured, shaking his head. "Let's get you to a more comfortable place."

Tasker carefully opened the door just wide enough for him to stick his arm in. Gripping Camry's upper arm, he held him steady as he opened it the rest of the way. Then he unbuckled his human's safety belt before sliding his arms under him and cradling his mate to his chest.

While Tasker wasn't that much larger than Camry, his paranormal strength made carrying him easy. He started across the garage, murmuring, "Thanks again, Gus."

"You're welcome, man." His brows drew together as he shook his head. "I sure hope you talk him into leaving that place soon, because it's a real dive."

Tasker sighed. "I know it is. I'll—"

Before more could be said, Tasker felt Camry stir in his arms. He kept half his attention on where they were going and the rest on his waking mate. To Tasker's surprise, as soon as Camry seemed half awake, he started to struggle.

Tasker began trilling even as he crooned words of comfort to his mate.

Camry's eyes finally snapped open, and he peered up at Tasker, his surprise clear.

"Hello, my mate," Tasker murmured, ceasing his trilling. "Welcome to the estate."

CHAPTER EIGHT

Camry couldn't believe he'd fallen asleep. He rarely slept in a vehicle to begin with — too uncomfortable. But to fall asleep in a stranger's truck, Camry must have been damn near exhausted.

"Um, hi," Camry replied uncertainly. He glanced left and right, having a hard time meeting the other man's gaze. Finally, Camry peered at him from beneath his lashes. "You, uh, you should have woken me."

"You looked so peaceful," Tasker told him with a smile. "I didn't have the heart to wake you."

"Well, um, I'm awake now," Camry pointed out needlessly. "You can put me down now. I can walk."

Tasker chuckled as he began climbing the stairs, making it look easy even though he still carried him. "No, my mate," he countered with a roguish grin. "I finally have you right where I want you. In my arms." With a wink, Tasker added, "I think I'll take advantage a little longer and keep holding you."

Camry opened his mouth, then closed it again, uncertain what to say to that.

"Just relax for another moment," Tasker urged him. "I'm almost there."

Since Camry didn't know what to say to get the gargoyle to release him — at least, not without hurting his feelings, which he found himself loath to do — he stayed quiet and relaxed against the gargoyle's chest. With his palm resting on Tasker's pectoral, he barely resisted the urge to pet the male. The gargoyle was built lean and muscular, although he was a little broader than Camry's own body, but he guessed there was so much hidden power within him.

"Turn the knob for me, will you?" Tasker asked, stopping before a familiar-looking door.

Camry noted that the room he'd used several nights before was right across the hall, so he knew he was about to open Tasker's door.

Am I ready for that step?

"Camry?" Tasker's single word held a wealth of concern. When Camry continued to hesitate, Tasker began to turn toward the opposite door as he said, "If you're not ready, we can—"

"No," Camry murmured, grabbing Tasker's door's knob. "I'm just nervous."

"I know you probably won't believe me," Tasker replied quietly as Camry opened the door and pushed it partway open. "But I am, too."

"How can that be?" Camry didn't understand. "I bet you've been with loads of guys. How can you be nervous?"

As Camry asked the question, he took in Tasker's suite. While the layout was similar to the room across the hall, there were plenty of homey touches, too. The room had been painted in shades of blue, there were throw pillows on the sofas, and a blanket lay folded on the back of the largest one.

There were a few seashells here and there as knickknacks.

Camry realized Tasker had remained silent, and he snapped his gaze up to the male's face.

That seemed to be what Tasker had been waiting for, as he pinned Camry with an intense expression. "I won't lie. I've been with more people than I can actually remember," Tasker told Camry bluntly. "But none of them were you, and *you* are everything to me."

"Wow." Camry couldn't think of anything else to say. Sometimes, the things Tasker said to him just took his breath away.

Tasker didn't seem to need a response. He used a foot to close his door before striding through the room. Turning right, he headed into the bathroom, which was definitely bigger than the one across the hall, since it sported that huge jetted tub Tasker had mentioned.

"When we first moved to this estate over a century ago," Tasker began saying as he placed Camry on the vanity. "The place was old and rundown. We each picked our suite, and we were given options on how to refurnish it." He leaned over and started the water running into the tub. Then he grabbed a bottle and squirted something into it. "I chose blues because I've never actually seen a blue sky, but I'm open to changing it if you want it decorated a different way."

"Why would you change it for me?" Camry asked, confusion filling him as he watched Tasker straighten and turn to face him once more.

Cocking his head, Tasker replied simply, "Because you're my mate, and I hope, someday, I'll convince you to live with me." A wry smile curved his blue lips as he added, "Mates live together after they bond, after all."

Then Tasker opened a cupboard and pulled out a bundle of fabric. "Here are some shorts. I'll leave you to change and get in on your own." After placing the item on the vanity next to his hip, Tasker told him, "Feel free to change the temperature if I didn't get it right. I'll be back in a few minutes after I change into shorts, too. I'll have some food with me, too. Are you allergic to anything?"

Camry shook his head. "Not allergic to anything." With a shrug, he added, "At least, nothing I've tried so far."

"Good." Tasker leaned forward and pecked a soft kiss to his lips. His dark eyes gleamed with want, but he pulled away from Camry. "I'll be back in a few. Get comfortable."

Then Tasker hurried from the bathroom, closing the door behind him.

After taking in a deep breath and letting it out just as slowly, Camry eased off the vanity. He knew what Tasker was doing by offering him space. The gargoyle had told him over and over that they would go at his speed.

The male was probably taking a moment to regain his own control.

Camry appreciated that. As much as he wanted to sit in the male's obviously strong arms and relax with him—maybe even accept some of that pampering Tasker mentioned—he didn't think he was ready for much more than that. With his experience being limited, Camry didn't have a frame of reference to fall back on.

Even his limited porn watching hadn't prepared Camry for someone as virile as Tasker seemed to be.

After shucking his clothes, folding them, and placing them on a chair, Camry pulled on the shorts. They covered more of him than the short-shorts at work, but not by much. They were also form-fitting, so if Camry hardened, he knew it would be clearly outlined.

At least that knowledge caused his burgeoning erection to die a swift death as nerves flooded him anew.

Camry did his best to push it out of his mind. Crossing to the tub, he bent and swished his hand through the pooling water. It was a little hotter than his taste, but he didn't mind.

Easing into the large tub, Camry realized that whatever Tasker had poured into the water made it feel silky smooth against his skin. The heat also began to relieve the soreness in his muscles nearly instantly. With a sigh, Camry rested against the curved back and stared at the ceiling.

After a moment, Camry wondered what was keeping Tasker. He was about to call out to the gargoyle, but his nerves got the better of him. Rubbing the water over his arms to distract himself, he continued to wait.

A moment later, the soft strains of music reached him. He

didn't recognize the style, which was filled with piano, soft vocalizations, and flute-like instruments. Whatever it was, he found it relaxing.

The door opened, revealing Tasker, who was pushing a small trolley laden with covered trays. After he'd positioned it beside the tub, he reached down and picked up a couple of things from the lower shelf. Tasker lifted them, revealing his offerings.

"I have bottled water, beer, wine, and the fireball whiskey you enjoyed before," Tasker shared, holding two in each hand. "What would you like?"

"I should really drink water," Camry stated on a groan. "But you're making it difficult to be good."

Chuckling, Tasker placed the bottle of water on the top of the cart. "Okay. After you drink that, what would you like to follow it up?"

Camry grinned. "The beer would be great." Then he noticed the label. "How did you know that was my favorite?"

Looking chagrined as he returned the fireball and wine to the lower shelf, Tasker admitted, "Gus overheard Morgan urging you to have a beer with him. He said the brand name and how it was your favorite." As Tasker removed the lids from the trays and set them aside, he explained, "Gus texted the info to me, and I found a couple of bottles in one of our bars."

"One of," Camry mused. "How many bars are in this estate?"

"Including the private one in the chieftain's office?" Tasker's eyes were narrowed, and he appeared to be doing a mental count, so Camry didn't respond. "Uh, seven, I think."

"Seven." Camry whispered the word, amazement flooding him. "It's impressive how you all live."

Tasker touched Camry's shoulder. "Will you ease forward so I can sit behind you?"

Camry complied, scooting forward in the tub.

Once Tasker was behind him, his blue legs bracketing Camry's own medium-brown ones, the contrast drawing his attention, Tasker gripped his upper arms and encouraged Camry to lean against him.

After Camry relaxed against Tasker's strong chest, the gargoyle whispered into his ear, "You could live this way, too, my mate." He pressed a kiss to Camry's neck before whispering, "I hope you'll take me up on my offer soon, but tonight, we'll relax, I'll pamper you, and I'll help you unwind and rest."

Relieved to hear that Tasker didn't expect too much to happen—*and I'm not disappointed*—Camry rested the back of his head against Tasker's shoulder. "Thanks, Tasker," he murmured. "This is . . . this is really, really nice. Thank you."

"Anything for you, my mate," Tasker replied huskily.

Then Tasker reached over and grabbed the water bottle. He twisted the cap, and Camry heard the distinctive pop of a seal being broken. When Tasker handed it to him, he didn't hesitate to accept it and bring the bottle to his lips.

The cold bottle felt good against the palm of Camry's hand and the water even better as it slid down his throat. He downed half of it in one go before resting it back on the edge of the tub. Tasker was immediately there, offering a small plastic plate filled with meats, cheeses, nuts, and seeds.

"No fruits?" Camry asked curiously as he picked up a piece of prosciutto-wrapped cheese.

"There's some up there if you want it," Tasker confirmed. "Green grapes and slices of apples. I wasn't certain if you'd want something with that much sugar, even natural sugar, this late at night before bed."

"Maybe a few of each, but you're right, I probably shouldn't have much," Camry conceded. Without thinking, before popping another bite into his mouth, he told Tasker, "I don't normally eat much of anything after work. I'm too tired to prepare it and not organized enough to do it beforehand."

"Hmmm," Tasker hummed, pecking the side of his neck. "How do you keep your weight up with all the exercise you do, then?"

Camry winced. "Think I'm underweight, Tasker?"

In truth, Camry was, and he knew it. He just wasn't underweight enough to worry about it.

Tasker shrugged, his shoulders moving behind Camry's. "I noticed because I want to know everything about you, not because I don't like the way you look." Nipping at Camry's neck, he rumbled huskily, "You should probably know, due to our heightened sense of smells, paranormals find attraction different than humans. We go by scent, so a person could be absolutely stunning by human standards, but if they didn't smell good or right, then we wouldn't be interested in them, even if they paraded themselves naked in front of us."

Chuckling at that visual, Camry tipped his head back so he could meet Tasker's gaze. "I think I like that," he admitted. "Because I did almost parade myself naked in front of you."

Tasker chuckled as he shook his head. "That wasn't quite what I meant, but I'm glad it pleases you." Then he dipped his head and pressed a lingering, sipping kiss to Camry's lips. He licked at Camry's bottom lip once, then groaned and lifted his head. "Drink your water. Eat the food. I'm trying to be good here."

Camry opened his mouth. It was on the tip of his tongue to tell Tasker that he didn't want good. Just as quickly, he thought better of it. Camry didn't want to lead the gargoyle on, after all.

Smiling and nodding, Camry picked up his water and finished the bottle. When he set it aside, Tasker was there instantly with the open bottle of beer. After murmuring his thanks, Camry ate a bit more of the meats and cheeses, then started on the walnuts, pecans, and sunflower seeds.

Once his plate was clean, Camry reached for the beer.

"Do you want more?" Tasker asked.

As Tasker spoke, he lifted a hand and trailed hot water over Camry's shoulder, creating warm rivulets of pleasure as it slid down his arm. His blood heated and began flowing to his groin. He felt his dick stir, hardening in his shorts. Considering his ass was pressed against Tasker's groin, he knew the gargoyle was in a similar state, and that knowledge seemed to make his own body respond that much faster.

"Maybe in a little bit," Camry replied, his voice coming out huskier than normal. "Gonna enjoy my beer first."

"Anything you want."

"Anything?" Camry couldn't help but ask.

"Well." Tasker suddenly sounded cautious. "Almost."

Camry's ardor cooled just a little as curiosity forced him to ask, "So, what's off the table?"

What would this experienced gargoyle refuse to do?

"Please don't ask me to walk away from you," Tasker murmured, a note of pleading in his tone. His voice grew rough for a reason that Camry guessed had nothing to do with arousal. "I can't do it, my mate. Now that I've met you." His arms tightened around Camry's torso, clutching him close as if Camry were suddenly preparing to flee. "You're everything to me."

The need to soothe Tasker rushed through Camry, and he quickly set down his beer. Sinking both arms into the water, he rested his hands over the gargoyle's forearms. He rubbed up and down them, massaging lightly.

"Hey, relax," Camry crooned, tipping his head back so he could meet Tasker's gaze. Seeing the concern in the male's deep green eyes, he quickly assured, "I may not be ready to let you fuck me, but I don't want to walk away. I just . . . need a little more time to work up to that."

"What about fucking me?" Then Tasker's eyes widened, and he grimaced. "Shit. I can be patient. Forget I said that."

Except, with the idea planted in Camry's head, he couldn't. "You'd let me fuck you?"

Tasker's blue eyebrow ridges furrowed. "Didn't we make that clear? Claiming has to be both ways." Then he shrugged. "Besides. I'm a switch. I love giving and receiving, and I hope that you'll end up that way, too." Rubbing over Camry's stomach, Tasker added, "There are so many wonderful positions for us to explore together. I look forward to every second of it."

Once again, Camry found himself whispering, "Wow."

CHAPTER NINE

"So, I guess you guys didn't really explain bonding to me."

Upon hearing Camry's softly spoken words, Tasker pulled his head out of the gutter. With his mate wet and nearly naked in his arms, it was difficult. He could smell Camry's arousal, but he knew he needed to ignore it . . . for now, anyway.

"How's it work?"

Well, shit.

They had missed a number of key points—one of them being male pregnancy.

I'll explain that soon.

As soon as Tasker had scented Camry, he'd begun eating cinnamon every day, so he knew he wasn't fertile. They had time for that one. Plus, if Camry never wanted children, Tasker could live with that.

While gargoyles didn't breed as prolifically as other species, so every hatchling was considered a gift, Tasker could take or leave younglings.

"Tasker?" Camry's voice sounded worried. "Did I ask something wrong?"

"No, not at all," Tasker assured, getting his head out of his ass and back to the matter at hand. "In order to bond, we both have to claim each other. The fastest way for a male-male pairing to do it is if we spill in each other and exchange bites."

"Uh, exchange *bites*?" Camry tensed in his arms.

Tasker nuzzled Camry's neck, licking and sucking for a moment, waiting for his mate to relax before speaking again.

"Yes, bites," Tasker confirmed before nipping at the thick tendon where his neck met his shoulder. "I'll sink my teeth into you right here," he told him, ignoring the way Camry once again began to tense. "And you'll orgasm from it."

Camry froze for a whole different reason. "I, uh, what?"

Chuckling softly, Tasker continued to nuzzle the human Fate had deemed his. "Yes, you heard right," he crooned. "You'll orgasm from it."

"Seriously?" Camry didn't sound convinced.

"Yes, seriously," Tasker confirmed. "In fact, I've heard that, after the first time, mates beg to be bitten again and again, although it's not needed to strengthen one's bond." He shrugged, hoping the day Camry would ask for such a thing would be soon. "It feels that good."

"Huh." Camry lifted an arm from the water and grabbed his beer. After taking a swig, he set it back down again. "That's . . . hard to believe, I guess."

"I know." Tasker wasn't going to force his mate to overthink it. "And I don't expect you to truly bite me, but you will need to drink a little of my blood to complete the exchange."

Camry nodded once. To Tasker's surprise, his mate stated, "Yeah, okay. I can do that."

"Most humans find the idea of blood consumption a bit . . . unsettling," Tasker pointed out.

Scoffing, Camry replied, "And when a person gets a paper cut and they start bleeding, what's the first thing most of them do?"

Tasker frowned. "Um, I don't know."

With a laugh, Camry peered over his shoulder at him. "They stick their finger in their mouth and suck on the wound." Shrugging, he added, "I figure it can't be any different than that, right?"

Chuckling right along with Camry, Tasker enjoyed the moment of relaxed mirth with his mate. "Gotcha. Interesting."

"So, anyway," Camry mused. "Exchange seed and blood. Then we'll be bonded."

"Right."

Camry sat in silence for a moment, the only sound filling the air the spa-style music Tasker had turned on for this very reason. Quiet moments wouldn't end up awkward.

"Um, is there anything else I should know about being bonded with a gargoyle?" Camry asked, his tone searching. "Uh, the guys make it seem like marriage, and I always wanted my partner to be faithful to me, so, um, maybe we should discuss that up front." Camry's voice became softer and softer the more he spoke. "I don't want to share you, but you said you've been with tons of people, so how could I manage to keep you happy for hundreds of years? You could get bored, and —"

Tasker clamped his hand over Camry's mouth to stop his words. He fought a full-body tremble as he struggled to get himself under control. The thought of sharing had struck a nerve with his instincts, and he knew he needed to address it. Tasker just needed to make certain his voice came out even when he did. Never did he want to snap at his mate.

"Hush a moment," Tasker finally managed to say, although he still growled a little. Then he lowered his hand back to Camry's waist and held him close. He tucked his face against the crook of his human's neck and inhaled deeply, drawing in the man's delicious natural aroma mixed with the bath oil. To Tasker's relief, Camry remained silent and pliant in his arms. When he felt in control, he lifted his head and whispered, "Mated paranormals don't stray. It's not even physically possible."

"Really?" Camry asked, his disbelief clear in his tone. "How's that work?"

"I mean, I'll never be able to get an erection for anyone but you, Camry," Tasker answered seriously. Lifting his hand, he gently cradled Camry's jaw and urged him to tip his head back. Once Tasker peered into Camry's dark eyes, seeing the shock there, he offered a small smile. "The hottest man or woman could jump on me naked, and it would do nothing for me." Waggling his brows, Tasker added, "Now, if you were to jump on me naked, I'd pin you to the wall and fuck us both stupid."

To Tasker's relief, just as he'd hoped, Camry barked a laugh. He grinned widely, flashing his white teeth. Nodding a smidge under his hand, Tasker took advantage and rubbed his thumb over Camry's full bottom lip, feeling the soft pad give slightly.

When Camry gently nipped him, Tasker groaned as heat flooded him. "Oh, Camry," he rumbled. "Good, remember?"

Grimacing, Camry nodded. "Right." He turned back around and relaxed in the circle of Tasker's arms once more. "So, about this exchanging fluid thing."

"Hmmm?" Tasker murmured, returning to nuzzling Camry's neck. He loved the way his mate tipped his head to the side, offering more of his lovely dark skin.

"How much fluid are we talking? Several orgasms or what?"

Tasker paused where he was playing with Camry's gorgeous flesh to really focus on his mate's question.

What exactly is he asking?

"Uh, well, I'm not one-hundred percent sure on that," Tasker admitted. "I've always heard that one orgasm between males is enough. I spill in you, you spill in me, bite each other, and that completes our bond." After a few seconds of hesitation, Tasker shared, "There are a few stories about how other couples have completed their bond. Couples where one person isn't comfortable bottoming. There are workarounds."

"Okay," Camry mused. "Theoretically, there are ways to

bond without you having to wait until I'm ready to bottom. I'll get there," he quickly added, turning to meet Tasker's gaze once more. "I'm just not there quite yet." With a soft scoff, Camry admitted, "A boyfriend or partner or whatever wasn't even a blip on my radar until I met you, but I've been dreaming about you and . . . god, what we do together in my dreams is so hot, I wake up hard and aching."

"Yeah," Tasker whispered, understanding. In truth, Fate used those dreams to urge a mate to accept their gargoyle, but he kept that little fact to himself. "I've been dreaming of you, too, baby."

"You have?" Camry sounded surprised.

"I have," Tasker confirmed.

Camry's smile appeared tentative. "Then . . . would you be open to trying to bond without fucking?" He quickly cleared his throat. "I mean either way. I'll fuck you eventually, too, but I don't want you to feel obligated to allow me to do something to you that I'm not ready for. I always believed a partnership should be an equal give and take."

As much as Tasker would love to beg his mate to fuck him, that he would love to feel his lover's rod spearing him, he bit back those words. Instead, he asked, "If we do this, I'll need you here every night, Camry." After a second of hesitation, he added, "And if you didn't need to pay for that apartment, you wouldn't need your job anymore. You could—"

Shaking his head, Camry pressed his palm over Tasker's mouth, shutting him up similarly to how Tasker had done the same to him. "I still need to earn money, Tasker," he told him. "I don't even know where you guys get your money from, and I won't be a freeloader." As Camry lifted his hand away, he added, "Besides, I've been taking college classes part-time, and I really want to continue. I don't want to live on credit, so it's taking longer, but I do want a degree."

"Okay." Tasker could concede that. "What are you getting

a degree in?"

"Hotel management," Camry told him. "Durango has plenty of hotels, so I figured I'd be able to put it to good use here."

Impressed, Tasker nodded. "Would you prefer to go to college full time?" When he saw the refusal coming a mile away, he quickly stated, "Not a loan. Not a gift. One partner caring for the other while helping them chase their dreams."

Camry hesitated. "I'll think about it."

Tasker would take that. "And moving in here?"

"It's awfully fast," Camry murmured.

That's not a no.

With a shrug, Tasker told him, "It's the way of the paranormal. We do things fast because we already know it'll be worth it in the end."

Finally, Camry nodded once. "I'll give my notice to my landlord tomorrow morning."

Doing a mental fist-pump, Tasker grinned broadly at Camry. "You have no idea how happy that makes me."

Waggling his eyebrows playfully, Camry teased, "I can think of a few ways we could end up happier."

Tasker nodded while letting out a chuckle. "Me, too." Sobering, he asked, "Am I pushing you, Camry? Yes, I want you with every fiber of my being, but I don't want you to regret this decision down the road."

"I'll only regret it if you turn out to be a lying asshole," Camry told him, his scent filled with honesty.

Blowing out a harsh breath, Tasker admitted, "I can't promise to never do something assholish, but I can promise that I didn't intend it that way." He shrugged, admitting, "We all make mistakes, and I've never been in a relationship, so I'm bound to screw up sometime."

"Everyone screws up sometime," Camry countered.

Tasker accepted that with a nod. "Okay." He swept his gaze over Camry's beautiful dark flesh, thinking about how to go about fulfilling his mate's request. "No fucking, obviously, but you must be comfortable with fingers, right?"

Camry's scent took on a slightly peppery scent that Tasker was coming to recognize as embarrassment.

"None of that, Camry," Tasker rumbled, gliding his hands up and down his arms. "We're mates, and I want to know everything about you." Smiling, he added, "I have a tail, and I love fucking myself with it. I'd like to show you a little of that enjoyment." Tasker slid his tail up Camry's muscular leg, drawing attention to his extra appendage. "And it's not any thicker than my fingers."

"Uh, okay," Camry finally murmured. "Yes. I finger myself."

Tasker noticed Camry still scented of embarrassment, but he didn't call attention to it. Instead, he nodded and asked, "How about we start with that massage, first?"

To Tasker's surprise, Camry shook his head. "Better not." Then he let out a jaw-cracking yawn before smiling sheepishly at Tasker. "Unless you intend to put me to sleep so we can try this another night."

"Gods, that wasn't what I was thinking at all," Tasker assured, shaking his head. "I was just trying to take care of your needs. I'm sure you're still sore."

Camry shrugged. "I'm used to being sore," he told him, which didn't really please Tasker. "But between whatever oil you put in the tub and the food and drink, I feel so much better than I normally do." After Camry obviously fought back another yawn, he told him, "But if we're going to do this, I need an activity that's going to raise my heart rate, not relax it."

Growling softly, Tasker nodded. Lust and need slammed into him, sending his arousal soaring. Still, he reined it in, keeping his touch light as he gently squeezed Camry's arm.

"Let's get out of here, dry off, and move to the bed." Tasker narrowed his eyes as his anticipation ramped up. "I can think of a number of ways to raise your heart rate."

"I'd hoped you could," Camry murmured, a husky note creeping into his voice.

Tasker gave up any pretense of subtlety. His mate was offering to bond. While it wouldn't be in the traditional way, they would get there. Tasker just hoped that what they were about to try did the trick.

Gripping Camry's waist, Tasker lifted his mate so he was standing in the water. He quickly followed, levering to his feet. He nearly slipped once in his excitement, but he caught himself. Then Tasker hurried from the tub.

After grabbing a towel, Tasker held it up to Camry, who was making his own way out of the water. He quickly wrapped up his human, although he didn't miss the beautiful erection trapped behind the shorts. In a similar state, Tasker wasn't shy about peeling off his own shorts.

Seeing how Camry bit his thick lower lip and glanced away, clutching his towel tight around him, Tasker yanked a second towel from the bar and wrapped it around his waist.

"I'll take this stuff back to the fridge for later," Tasker told Camry, gripping the trolley's handle. "Meet me in the bedroom when you're ready."

Unable to help himself, Tasker had to touch. He gently cradled Camry's jaw and eased closer to him. Ever-so-lightly, he touched his lips to his mate's. Tasker lapped lightly along Camry's lower lip.

When Camry opened to him, Tasker intended to just take a quick taste—a sample, as it were. Except, as soon as his mate's flavor burst across his taste buds, he groaned and his arousal surged. Tasker wrapped his second arm around the man's waist while using his hold on his jaw to deepen the kiss, thrusting in his tongue.

Reveling in the exquisite taste of everything Camry, Tasker

mapped his mate's mouth. He lapped and teased at the other man's tongue. When Camry began to kiss him back, Tasker nearly exploded just from that simple pleasure. His cock throbbed, and his hips jerked, applying much-needed pressure to his erection.

Realizing what he did, Tasker groaned as he broke the kiss. He rested his forehead against Camry's, panting hard. To his pleasure, he found his mate in an answering state, and for several seconds, they stood in each other's arms, sharing breaths.

"Wow," Tasker muttered finally. Grinning, he eased away from his man. "Kissing you is . . . beyond description."

"I-Is everything we do together going to be that . . . intense?" Camry asked.

Nodding once, Tasker stated, "I believe so."

When Camry didn't respond right away, Tasker turned back to the trolley and the waiting food and drink. "See you out there." Then he hurried from the room, giving them both a chance to gather a little self-control.

As if that can happen with my mate in my arms.

Tasker continued to smile widely as he put everything away.

CHAPTER TEN

Still panting, Camry watched Tasker exit the bathroom. He lifted one hand and touched his fingertips to his lips. Camry had never been kissed like that before, and he hoped that each time they came together, it would always feel like that.

Time will tell.

Camry quickly shucked his soaked shorts, then dried himself. After that, he wrapped the towel back around his waist. Even though he stripped several nights a week, he couldn't bring himself to just strut out there naked.

Instead, Camry felt a fresh bout of nerves coming on. He didn't know what had come over himself to make such an offer to Tasker. While Camry knew the gargoyle wanted him — his erection digging into his back had been a dead giveaway — he'd known he wasn't ready to fuck quite yet.

That hadn't stopped Camry from wanting everything that Tasker was offering him.

If this works, I can have it, too.

Girding up his courage, Camry headed out of the room. He peered to the left, into the bedroom, and he didn't know if he felt relief or disappointment. Instead of seeing his naked soon-to-be lover on clear display, Camry saw that Tasker had kept his towel around his waist, too. Tasker had even pushed the comforter and top sheet down, sliding his feet underneath it.

God, I'm being ridiculous. He's just being thoughtful.

"I wasn't certain if you wanted to cuddle under the blanket

as we explore," Tasker offered, pointing at the aforementioned item. "It could get messy, though, because kissing seems to make us lose our heads fast enough."

Camry chuckled softly as he nodded. "That's for sure."

He couldn't say he minded, though. It was a clear indicator of the chemistry between them. He'd never felt anything so intense, and he wanted to feel that again.

Stopping at the side of the bed, Camry hesitated. Then he slowly reached for the towel. With his hand hovering over his waist, he took a fortifying breath.

Then Camry let the towel drop.

Unable to meet Tasker's gaze, even when the gargoyle groaned in obvious appreciation, Camry still focused on the sheet. He did manage to force his body to move forward, though. Lifting his leg, Camry climbed on the mattress.

Immediately, Tasker wrapped his arms around him. He guided him forward, bringing their bodies together.

At some point when Camry wasn't looking, Tasker had pushed his own towel aside. Everywhere they touched, it was just skin on skin. His body flushed hot from the wonderful sensation of it.

Groaning softly, Camry murmured Tasker's name as he stretched out beside the gargoyle. The feel of his slightly bumpy, mottled hide sent his senses soaring even higher. His mind began to blank, and he couldn't think of anything to say as he rutted his erection against Tasker's flesh.

"That's the way," Tasker crooned into Camry's ear. "Move, baby. Show me how you like it."

Camry moaned Tasker's name again. It seemed to be the only thing that would make it past his throat. He felt Tasker's palms slide down his arms to his torso, settling on his waist. Then Tasker urged him sideways a little.

In seconds, Camry found himself straddling Tasker's

waist. For the first time in his life, he felt another male's erection against his own, and he couldn't resist rutting against that hard length. His balls felt heavy and achy, and his shaft throbbed.

Tasker wrapped one arm around the back of Camry's shoulders, keeping their chests pinned together as if concerned that he would attempt to draw away. The gargoyle had his other arm around his waist, cupping one of his ass cheeks. He massaged Camry's globe rhythmically as he rocked in counterpoint with him, sending even more stimulation through Camry's body.

He would have been embarrassed by how quickly he was approaching the edge, but he heard Tasker's heavy breathing and soft grunts, telling him that his gargoyle was right there with him.

Yeah, he's mine.

"I'm yours," Tasker muttered into Camry's ear, telling him he'd said the words out loud.

That was okay. Camry didn't mind. The possessive notion seemed to spur him to even greater heights, and a tingle teased at the base of his spine. He knew his orgasm approached, and he could do nothing to stop it.

"Tasker," Camry grunted as his release swept over him. His body trembled and rocked in Tasker's hold, and he felt grateful for the male's arms. If the gargoyle released him, Camry just knew he would float away from the bliss of it.

Camry soared, flying on the endorphins from his release. Absently, he noticed the increased heat and felt Tasker's body jolt beneath him. Smiling and humming, Camry knew the gargoyle had come, too.

Huh. Maybe I don't need loads of experience to please him after all.

"No, you don't need experience to please me," Tasker purred into his ear. "All I need is you in my arms, and I'm beyond ecstatic."

Chuckling, Camry tipped his head a little so he could peer into Tasker's brilliant green eyes. "I keep saying stuff out loud." Wincing, he admitted, "I don't mean to."

"It's okay, my mate," Tasker countered, lifting a hand to gently scratch at his scalp. "I like knowing what's in your head."

Camry nodded absently, pushing into the stimulating touch.

"Ready for another orgasm?" Tasker asked huskily.

Camry eased open eyelids he hadn't realized he'd closed. "You really think your bite will get me off?" He wasn't a real big fan of pain.

Tasker nodded once, holding his gaze. "I do." He hesitated a few seconds before adding, "Trust me."

After swallowing hard, Camry tipped his head to the side. "I trust you." While Camry wasn't certain how it had happened—everything with Tasker was going at the speed of lightning—Camry knew his words were true. "Claim me."

Groaning with desire, Tasker lifted his mouth to Camry's neck. He licked and sucked on the flesh where his neck met his shoulder. The gargoyle mumbled his name, his tone so reverent it was quickly causing Camry's blood to heat anew.

Then . . . Camry felt it—sharp teeth against his skin. He nearly jerked away on instinct, just managing to stay the reaction. He couldn't help but tense, though.

Just as Camry feared, a flash of pain burst through his neck. His first thought was that, whoever had told Tasker that the claiming bite caused pleasure was full of shit. Then the most unexpected thing happened. Tingles erupted from where Tasker was sucking on his flesh. They coursed down his chest, causing his nipples to bead. When they passed his stomach, his muscles quivered with pleasure. Finally, they centered in his balls.

Camry's testicles pulled up so fast that he barely had time

to shout his pleasure before he was coming all over them both once more. Each sucking pull to his neck felt as if it transferred straight to his cock. If Camry had ever had a blowjob, he just knew that this was what it would feel like . . . only better.

Finally, when spots danced across his vision and a whine escaped Camry's throat, Tasker eased his teeth from his neck. Even the way the gargoyle lapped over his skin, cleaning it, caused more pleasant tingles, and his dick gave one more half-hearted spurt.

"Your turn, my mate."

Upon hearing Tasker's comment, Camry forced his head up. He met his gargoyle's gaze. When the male showed him his bleeding wrist, revealing that he'd cut himself and was offering Camry his blood, he balked and shook his head.

"No, that's not right."

Tasker's eyes widened, and his look was so crest-fallen, that Camry felt as if he'd been stabbed.

Sucking in a harsh breath, Camry forced movement into his limbs. "I mean, it should be like this," he declared as he positioned his face at Tasker's neck, mirroring what his gargoyle had done to him.

Camry opened wide and wrapped his jaw around the point of the gargoyle's shoulder. He bit . . . hard. It took much more pressure than he'd anticipated, but finally, he felt his teeth pierce Tasker's skin.

To Camry's surprise, as Tasker's blood flowed across his tongue, he found it tasted really good. He licked around his teeth, lapping up more. As Camry sucked, he felt Tasker's body jolt and heard his deep moan in his ear.

After several more laps across Tasker's skin, Camry eased his teeth from his flesh. He spotted the blood continuing to well up from his mark and lapped over them to clean them. Camry watched in fascination as a scar quickly formed where he'd bitten, and to his surprise, a wealth of smug satisfaction filled him.

That's my mark.

Lifting his head, Camry took in Tasker's heavy-lidded expression and parted lips. He looked absolutely stunning while blissed out from his orgasms. Camry dipped his head and pecked a kiss to those parted lips.

"Mmmm," Tasker rumbled huskily. "You're incredible, my mate."

Camry basked in the praise, overjoyed that he'd pleased his gargoyle so thoroughly.

"Now," Tasker murmured, holding his gaze. "I'm going to see about inserting some of our fluids into both our asses." For a second, he hesitated before asking, "Are you okay with that?"

Camry nodded quickly, more than on board with that, and he spread his legs wider while getting his knees under him. The move opened his cheeks, but he refused to feel self-conscious. This was the man who was going to be by his side for the rest of his life.

The new position also slightly separated their bodies, giving Tasker room to work. He quickly did just that, too. Tasker slid his tail between them.

As Camry watched, Tasker scooped up a generous dollop with his tail.

"How much control do you have over your tail?" Camry asked curiously as he felt the appendage prod his entrance.

Camry realized he probably should have asked that before.

"Total control," Tasker answered with a quiet growl in his voice.

At the same time, Tasker pushed his tail into Camry's body, the mix of seed coupled with the silkiness of the oil that had been in the bathwater making it glide in quite easily. Just as it began to stretch Camry's chute a little more than he was used to, Tasker twisted his appendage and nailed Camry's prostate.

Sparks shot through Camry's rectum and groin, and he moaned with pleasure.

"Yeah, there it is," Tasker crooned. He hit Camry's gland once more before withdrawing his tail.

Camry groaned, that time at the loss of stimulation.

Tasker chuckled huskily. "Hang on, baby," he crooned. "Just getting more."

For several minutes, Tasker played with Camry's ass, pushing more and more seed into him while pegging his prostate with each pass. Finally, it became too much. Camry felt his balls draw tight, and before he could even think of controlling himself, Camry anointed Tasker's body with a third load of jizz.

Dark spots flashed across Camry's vision, and his arms and legs trembled as his body shook.

"Easy, my mate," Tasker murmured into his ear as he helped him sideways. "Just relax. I'll take care of everything." Camry couldn't force his eyes open as he felt Tasker press a kiss to his forehead. "Gonna fill my ass with your seed real quick. Then I'll clean us both up."

Camry tried to grunt his acceptance, but he wasn't certain he pulled it off. The pull of sleep was too great, and he drifted into oblivion.

CHAPTER ELEVEN

Tasker had known going through molt was painful. He'd expected it. Never could he have anticipated just *how* painful it was, though.

Being told, warned, and experiencing it were two totally different things.

Fortunately, Tasker had learned another trick from those who'd found their mates before him—keep said mate close, literally. When Tasker's molt began, he eased a still-sleeping Camry onto his chest. Everywhere his lover touched him dulled the fiery tendrils.

Tasker had almost completed the change before Camry began to rouse. His human had hummed and turned his head, then just about fallen off of him in obvious shock. Tasker had tightened his hold, keeping him in place.

"Easy, my mate," Tasker mumbled roughly. "It's still me. Going through molt." He had to pause to clench his teeth so he didn't scream when his wings retracted into his back for the first time. Panting, Tasker offered Camry a wan smile. "There. Done."

"Holy shit, that sounded painful," Camry commented, sweeping his gaze over Tasker over and over. "So, uh, wow." Cocking his head, he pinned him with a wry smile. "I sorta miss the blue."

Chuckling softly, Tasker felt a wealth of relief. "I'm glad you like my true form, too. I was worried." He grimaced, realizing the pain must have loosened his tongue.

"You were worried?" Camry began smoothing his hair

away from his face. "Why?"

Tasker could see that his white locks had deepened to a pale golden-yellow. As much as he wondered what the rest of him looked like, he didn't have the energy to get up and look. Even though he was sweaty from the pain of molt, Tasker really just wanted to roll over, wrap his mate in his arms, and go back to sleep.

"Why were you worried?" Camry pressed.

Forcing himself to focus, Tasker reminded him, "I told you how paranormals feel attraction differently than humans?" After seeing Camry nod, he continued, "Well, what if you didn't find me attractive as a gargoyle?"

Camry scoffed. "That makes no kind of sense." He shook his head as he eyed him. "Then why would I agree to bond with you?"

Shrugging, Tasker offered, "So I'd have a human form that you would like better."

"Well, I'm attracted to you in both forms," Camry declared before ordering, "so you just get that idea right out of your head."

A jaw-cracking yawn interrupted Camry, making Tasker smile.

"Yes, my mate," Tasker replied, pecking a kiss to Camry's lips. "And yes, it was painful." After a few seconds of hesitation, he added, "It's still very early, yet. Just sunrise. How about we go back to sleep for a little while?"

"Yes, please," Camry muttered, his eyes already drifting closed. He eased off of Tasker's body and curled into his side.

Tasker smiled as he held Camry close and drifted off to sleep right along with him.

Heading into Camry's apartment building, Tasker tried not to growl upon seeing the elevator's *out of order* sign. He'd known the old building would be shabby, but the place was four stories. Basic maintenance should have been upkept.

Camry either didn't hear him or he ignored it as he led not only Tasker but Mitch, Aaden, Andre, and their men up the stairs to the third floor. Aziel had wanted to come, too, but he'd already made plans with his brother. Evidently, they were going apartment hunting.

Go figure.

From what Tasker had heard, Aziel's brother Aaron hadn't met with Maelgwn, yet. The man didn't know that there could possibly be a place for him there. Aziel had admitted that he was going with Aaron simply to try to stall the man's decision.

Aaron was supposed to go to a barbeque at the estate in a few days, and Maelgwn was going to vet the man then.

Upon reaching the third floor, Camry led the way inside. He looked a little uncomfortable as he glanced around what had been his home for the last several months — or so Camry had told him. The one-bedroom was open-concept with only the bedroom, a coat closet, and the bathroom behind closed doors.

"Um, yeah," Camry began. "So, it shouldn't take me long at all to get everything together."

"Please tell me we don't have to hike the furniture downstairs, too," Aaden muttered, already rubbing his back.

Grigoris chuckled before pecking a kiss to his mate's neck. "Are you angling for a massage, my love?"

Aaden waggled his eyebrows. "Is it working?"

With a growl, Grigoris rumbled, "Anytime."

Aaden's friends laughed, and Tasker couldn't help but smile. Seeing Grigoris with his mate was like seeing a whole different gargoyle. The male had always been curt and standoffish, wanting nothing to do with anyone unless it involved talking to them about their vehicles.

With Aaden, Grigoris was downright sweet.

Of course, Tasker would never be stupid enough to actually say that to the gargoyle's face.

"Uh, no, fortunately," Camry stated. "The furniture stays. This place came furnished. The only thing I bought was a mattress."

Considering the comments Camry had made about not only Tasker's mattress but the one that had been in the guest room and how wonderful he found them, Tasker sure hoped his mate hadn't paid much for the mattress he'd bought.

"And I'm not going to take that, either," Camry continued with a chuckle. "No sense in that when Tasker's is about ten times better."

Tasker grinned, pleased with the praise.

As Tasker taped together a couple of the boxes they'd brought, Camry began moving things around. He placed the items he wanted to take on the sofa, and the rest of the guys packed them. Soon, the main room was done, and they only had two boxes.

"Nothing from the kitchen?" Tasker asked curiously.

Camry shrugged. "Uh, do you cook?"

"Not a lick," Tasker admitted. "I just work in the kitchen." He'd explained how mundane chores were rotated, so not everyone got stuck doing the same thing all the time. "And the laundry room."

"Well, I'm good too then." With a chuckle, Camry admitted, "The dining hall food is amazing."

"That it is. Our chefs are awesome," Sumak agreed with a wide smile. "I used to work in there, but I'm a guard now." Taking Andre's hand, the small gargoyle purred, "It's how I met my Andre."

"Best night jogging of my life," Andre replied, eyeing Sumak with barely concealed lust.

"Okay, okay." Kardamon lifted his hands and waved. "Let's get this over with so we can all get back to the estate and fuck."

As most of the others laughed, Tasker gave Camry a warm smile and a soft kiss, silently letting his mate know that they would get around to it when his mate was good and ready.

An hour later, Camry's stuff was loaded in the back of one of the estate's pick-up trucks, and his mate led the way toward the building manager's door.

Tasker really didn't like how nervous Camry suddenly appeared.

After knocking, his mate rocked from foot to foot as he rubbed his palms over the thighs of his jeans.

"Hey, easy," Tasker murmured, taking his hand and giving it a squeeze. "What's wrong? Talk to me."

"I—" Camry began, but the door swung open before he could finish.

A tall, severe-looking woman stared imperiously out at them. Her thin lips curved into a tight frown as she glanced from where Tasker held Camry's hand, then between them.

"Yes, Mister Palcha?" she asked sharply.

Camry held out the paper on which he'd written his notice. "I came to drop off my notice. I'm moving in with my boyfriend."

Tasker's heart warmed upon hearing those words.

Then he barely kept from grinding his teeth in annoyance when the woman read the paper and sniffed with disdain. "You have two months left on your six-month lease, Mister Palcha. Have you found a new tenant to take your place?"

The way she said his name made it sound as if she thought he was dirty.

"No, ma'am," Camry replied, subdued.

"Well. You'll be forfeiting your security deposit, then," she replied haughtily. Then she pinned her cold gaze on Tasker and asked with fake nonchalance, "Has Mister Palcha told you he's a stripper? He takes his clothes off for money."

Yep. She definitely thinks my mate's dirty.

Well, how about this, Miss High And Mighty?

Grinning broadly, Tasker stated, "Camry didn't have to tell me. That's where I met him." He lifted his mate's hand to his lips and kissed the back of it. "Couldn't take my eyes off him." With a fake laugh, Tasker returned his attention to the building manager. "You have no idea how pleased I was to find out his real name isn't Mongo."

Giving them a scandalized look, she curled her lip. "If that will be all, and don't expect a reference when you need another place," she tacked on coldly, as if it was a foregone conclusion that Tasker would kick Camry to the curb before too long.

Never gonna happen, lady.

"He won't need it," Tasker replied glibly. "Gonna put a ring on my man's finger as soon as I can convince him." While Camry stared at him in wide-eyed shock, Tasker realized he would have to address that comment before too long. *Oops. Later.* Instead, Tasker grinned at the lady again and stated, "Saw your elevator was out. Better get that fixed before a city inspector drops by."

Then Tasker wrapped his arm around Camry's waist and guided him away from the toxic, judgmental woman.

When he heard the door slam behind them, he grinned and winked at Camry.

"Did you just sort of propose to me?" Camry asked, sounding dazed.

Tasker didn't answer until they'd settled in the back seat of an estate SUV, and Grigoris had eased the vehicle onto the road. Turning on the back bench seat, he took both of Camry's hands between his own. He saw a mixture of hope and disbelief in his lover's eyes.

"Gargoyles don't usually bother with marriage because our bond is stronger than any piece of paper the state could give us," Tasker admitted. Seeing the hope in Camry's brown eyes dim, he quickly added, "But if you want to get married, I'll throw you the biggest damn wedding you could ever want." Lifting one of Camry's hands to his lips, Tasker bussed a kiss over it before saying, "You're my mate, Camry. I want you happy."

"What would make you happy?" Camry countered.

Chuckling, Tasker replied, "Making you happy makes me happy."

Camry rolled his eyes. "That's not an answer."

"It actually is as simple as that," Grigoris stated from the font of the vehicle, having obviously overheard. "When our mates are happy, we're happy. End of story."

When Camry glanced around the cab, everyone was nodding.

"Wow," he whispered.

Tasker left it at that. Grinning, he tucked his mate against his side and relaxed in the seat, happy to be on their way home.

Yep. Home with my mate.

Once again, Tasker was finding himself fighting possessive rage. He watched Camry twist and shimmy around the pole. His mate thrust his hips and whipped off another layer of what Tasker had been told was six thongs.

Camry never ever removed that last one.

It wasn't the fact that Camry was dancing nearly naked that was upsetting Tasker, either. This was where he'd met the man so that would have been hypocritical.

Instead, Tasker seethed due to the fact that someone had applied make-up to cover up his claiming scar on Camry's neck.

"You need to calm down," Tobias urged.

Tasker tried to do as the second ordered, but he was having a hell of a time succeeding. He knew if he didn't manage it, he was in danger of returning to his true form right there in the middle of the strip club. Tasker knew that would be a very, very bad thing.

Gripping his beer bottle with one hand, Tasker focused on deep breathing as he frowned at the table.

The second's hand on his shoulder certainly helped.

"Guess strippers aren't supposed to have noticeable scars," Tasker muttered, wondering why Camry had never said anything about that. He hoped it was because he hadn't known.

"I'm sure he was forced to do it by his asshole boss," Mitch tossed out, scowling off to the right. "Shit. That handsy rich dick is here again."

"That's why I'm here," Tobias stated.

"You knew Morgan would be here tonight?" Tasker asked, snapping his attention to where Mitch continued to stare. "Shit."

Spotting the expression of open lust on Morgan's face as he watched Camry perform, Tasker once again focused on the table. He understood the screaming people up front, who were jumping up and down while waving and throwing money. They just wanted to see a good show, and they appreciated Camry's hot body.

Morgan, however, his expression told a different story. The man didn't just appreciate Camry. Morgan wanted to possess Camry . . . like an object.

"Partly due to him, and partly due to this being your first time here as a bonded couple," Tobias revealed, once again squeezing his shoulder. "I wanted to check Morgan out first hand, and I also wanted to be certain you could handle watching your mate perform."

Nodding, Tasker muttered, "I appreciate it."

Looking back toward the stage, Tasker realized he'd missed the last couple of minutes of Camry's performance. A brunette woman was now working the pole.

Tasker watched the entrance to backstage, waiting for Camry to appear and make his required thirty-minute round. When several minutes passed and he didn't appear, unease slithered through him.

Where is Camry? Where is my mate?

Even as Tasker was thinking those words, Mitch asked another question. "Hey, where'd sleaze-ball go?"

"Shit," Tasker snarled, jumping to his feet. "Something's wrong."

As Tasker rushed through the club to the back, he ignored the owner hollering that he wasn't allowed back there. The bouncer was handled neatly by Tobias. Following his senses, Tasker easily found his mate's dressing room.

While the place was drenched in his lover's smell, that wasn't all that was there. A couple of other scents were there, too. What wasn't there, was his mate.

The room was empty.

Tasker flicked out his tongue and tasted the air, determined to track down his mate.

I just found him damn it.

CHAPTER TWELVE

After his show, Camry retreated to his room as always. He still seethed at Carlton's high-handed insistence that he use make-up to cover Tasker's scar. While Camry felt nothing but pride to bear his gargoyle's mark, when Carlton had seen it, his boss had been livid.

"You allowed some fuck to bite you hard enough to leave a mark?" Carlton had yelled. "Cover it with make-up at once." Curling his lip, he'd added, "No one wants to see a scarred stripper."

Then Carlton had stormed out of the room. He'd returned a couple of minutes before the show to confirm that Camry had done as he'd ordered. When Camry hadn't, Carlton had stood in the dressing room and watched as he'd done it, threatening to fire him if he refused.

It had been on the tip of Camry's tongue to say to hell with it all and shout, "So fire me." It would have felt so gratifying. Then Camry had recalled his insistence to Tasker that he needed his own money to pay for college, so he'd stuck it out.

As Camry washed down after his show, careful not to remove the make-up from his shoulder or he would just have to reapply it, Camry thought about how upset Tasker had appeared at his table. White-hot guilt filled Camry because he knew it had been he who'd caused it.

No job is worth this.

Camry pulled on his short-shorts and tank top, deciding this would be his last show. He would rather flip burgers, and now that he didn't have rent, he could make a minimum wage job work.

Let's just get through tonight.

With that thought in mind, Camry slipped on his boots. Just as he reached for the doorknob, the door was pushed open. He had to jump back a couple of feet to keep from getting hit in the face.

Ice rushed through his veins when he spotted Morgan Clarence standing on the other side.

Doing his best to appear unaffected by the creepy smile on the slender man's blond features, Camry stated, "I'm sorry, Mister Clarence, but this area is for employees only." Pointing toward the front, he offered, "I'll escort you. Are you at your regular booth?"

"Oh, don't worry, Mongo," Morgan answered silkily. "I have permission to be here, and we won't be returning to the front." Before Camry even realized what was happening, Morgan had grabbed his upper arm and began tugging him down the hall. "We'll be heading out the back. My car is waiting."

Twisting in Morgan's grip did no good, but Camry gave it his best shot anyway. "Let go of me," he cried, tugging against the man, but it felt as if he were trying to fight the tide.

"No, Mongo," Morgan countered, continuing to tug him along. "I've been more than patient, and it's time to make you mine. I can't wait for you to dance for me and only me."

"What the fuck?" Camry screamed. "What the hell is the matter with you?"

Morgan's eyes appeared to flash red, and when he grinned, his canines were sharp like . . . fangs.

"Vampire," Camry hissed, fear slicing through him.

Before meeting Tasker, Camry would never have guessed that vampires actually existed. His lover had explained that most were law-abiding citizens, similar to everyone else. Their need to consume blood made them a little unique, but they had rules, just like every paranormal group.

Except, Camry didn't think this guy followed those rules . . . not if he was kidnapping him against his will.

"Ah, you know of our kind. Excellent." Morgan seemed inordinately pleased. "Then it will be all the more fun to play with your mind because you'll understand what's happening but won't be able to resist."

As the irises of Morgan's normally gray eyes bled to red, a fresh wave of fear spiked through Camry.

Morgan smiled, the look creepy on what should have been handsome features. Except, Camry had always found the man off-putting, and now he understood why. His innate fight or flight reflex was alive and well and had pegged Morgan as a predator to be avoided.

"You will walk quietly by my side and get into the car with me," Morgan ordered, pinning Camry with a dark look. "You will not complain. Your body will respond to me as you've never responded to another."

Even as an odd coldness seemed to brush against Camry's brain, his mind chanted, "No, no, no."

Feeling Morgan's grip loosen — he obviously expected to be obeyed — Camry wrenched backward. For an instant, he managed to slip free. Camry tried to sprint back down the hall.

Morgan was far faster. When he grabbed Camry's arm again, stopping his momentum with a hard lurch, pain shot through his shoulder, and he feared it had been jerked from its socket. Fortunately, as he was propelled toward the back door once more, the pain ebbed.

"So," Morgan mused. "You are impervious to mental manipulation. Fascinating."

He opened the back door and bodily lifted Camry inside. Before Camry could scramble across the seat and open the opposite side's door, escaping that way, Morgan was in the cab and closing his door. The vampire gripped his leg and tugged him back toward him.

"It's rare, you know," Morgan continued as if they were having an everyday conversation. "Only about one percent of all humans are immune to our abilities."

The car started to move, and a fresh wash of fear cascaded through Camry. He was being kidnapped by a mad vampire.

How will Tasker find me?

"But I admit, it's been some time since I've had the opportunity of truly breaking a human's mind." Morgan gripped Camry's shoulder and forced him to turn and look at him. "No one's found any definitive proof of why a small handful are immune to—"

Morgan's thumb slid across the make-up, removing some of it, and he snapped his mouth shut. His eyes narrowed as he rubbed more of the concealer off of Camry's skin. His nostrils flared, and he curled his lip into a snarl.

"Who marked you?" Morgan demanded, his voice lowering to a lethal-sounding hiss. "Who would dare mark what is mine?"

"I'm *not* yours," Camry declared, going for bravado that he didn't feel. "I'm the mate of a gargoyle, and he's going to be coming after you." When he saw the contempt in Morgan's eyes, Camry quickly added, "Him and his whole clutch."

"No one will ever know where you've gone, Mongo," Morgan countered. "You will disappear, and now, I know I'll be able to enjoy you for centuries."

Oh shit.

Camry racked his brain for some counter, something that would make the vampire think his only means of escape was to release him, but he was coming up empty.

As Morgan began to chuckle cruelly, something heavy slammed into the side of the sedan. The car rocked sideways, swerving. The driver managed to right it only for something to hit the vehicle again.

Forcing a smile of his own, Camry taunted, "Did you forget about a gargoyle's mad tracking skills? My mate was at the club tonight. And now . . . he's here to stop you."

As if to punctuate Camry's words, the sound of a tire blowing blasted through the air. The car swerved once more before the driver brought it to a screeching stop. A second later, the vehicle rocked as something landed on top. Then a set of white claws pierced the roof, and it was peeled away like the lid of a sardine can.

To Camry's abject relief, he peered up into Tasker's enraged features.

"Give me my mate, vampire," Tasker ordered, his great white wings beating the air, causing a breeze to wash over them. It also caused Tasker's shoulder-length white hair to swirl around his head wildly. "And perhaps you'll live to suck another day."

"Or maybe." Morgan grabbed Camry's upper arm with one hand and lifted three-inch talons, which he'd grown from his fingertips, to Camry's neck. "I'll kill him, and you'll die a slow, agonizing death from heart-sickness."

Oh shit. That's not a thing, is it?

Camry didn't remember hearing about that.

Tasker let out a low, feral-sounding growl, and he flexed his white-clawed fingers.

Before either could say more, a dart whizzed by and embedded itself in Morgan's chest. The vampire's grip immediately loosened. He plucked the dart from his chest, but when he started to speak, his words were slurred.

"Wha—"

"Tranq dart, Morgan," Tobias stated, flying into view. "There's some Vampire Council enforcers that have been looking for you."

"No," Morgan whispered even as he toppled sideways.

"Yes," Tobias declared with a smirk.

Tasker swooped into the ruined cab and plucked Camry into his arms. Cradling him to his chest, he rose higher in the air. "My beautiful mate," Tasker rumbled. "Are you okay?

Are you injured?"

Unwilling to lie to Tasker, Camry admitted, "I'll have a few bruises, but nothing that won't fade quickly."

Letting out a wounded sound, Tasker cried, "I'm sorry I didn't get here sooner."

"But you did get here," Camry assured, rubbing his palms over Tasker's chest. "And you saved me."

In truth, Camry didn't even know where *here* was. They were on a dark, deserted road with trees on either side. It could have been any backroad in or around Durango.

"How is he?" Tobias asked, flapping his wings to fly next to them. "Should I message Doctor Perseus that you'll be stopping in?"

Camry quickly shook his head before Tasker could answer. "I'll be okay," he claimed. "Nothing a shower and a good night's rest won't cure." As Tobias began to nod, Camry asked, "What about the driver? Did he get away?"

Shaking his head, Tobias pointed.

Following the direction of his finger, Camry spotted a large red gargoyle carrying a man slung over his shoulder. He followed Einan, who carried an unconscious Morgan. Both disappeared amidst the trees, probably flying back to the gargoyle's estate.

"He was a vampire, too," Tobias revealed. "Another rogue." Shaking his head, he grumbled, "We'd cleared out a coven over a decade ago, and now these guys. Guess we'll have to do another sweep of the area." His features relaxing, Tobias made shooing motions at Tasker. "Take him home, Tasker. Give him that shower he wants."

"Wait," Camry cried, gripping Tasker's forearm tightly as his lover rotated in mid-air. "What about Carlton?"

"What about him?" Tobias asked.

"Morgan said he had permission to be in the back," Camry explained. "And he's the one who made me cover Tasker's claiming mark. He had to have known something was up."

There was no other explanation.

Tobias hummed, scratching his chin. "Okay. I'll look into it," he assured. "We already know he's an asshole, but selling humans to vampires is a whole different thing."

Camry shivered as Tobias voiced what he'd only been thinking. "Thank you, sir."

Tobias nodded. "See you at the estate."

Then Tasker flapped his wings, and the wind whipped past Camry as he rushed them home.

Before long, Tasker returned them to the estate. Instead of using the front door, he landed on a balcony. When he opened one of the French doors, Camry realized they were in Tasker's suite.

Our suite, now.

Tasker didn't even put him down until they were in the bathroom. After turning on the shower water, he stripped Camry with swift, precise scrapes of his claws. In seconds, Camry stood in nothing but his boots. For those, Tasker knelt and carefully pulled them from his feet before guiding him into the shower.

Finally, under the spray, Tasker spoke. "I feared I'd lost you," he whispered, cupping Camry's jaw. "I don't ever want to feel that way again." As a muscle ticked in his jaw, Tasker's voice came out tortured. "Please don't go back to work there."

"I'd already decided to quit," Camry assured his clearly troubled gargoyle. "I'd almost walked out when Carlton ordered me to cover your mark."

Rubbing his palms over Tasker's pectorals, Camry spotted the hungry gleam in his gargoyle's green eyes as he roved them over Camry's body. It suddenly hit him. He knew what his gargoyle needed.

"Do you have waterproof lube?"

For a few seconds, Tasker appeared confused. He blinked

once, twice, and his expression cleared. "Uh, yes."

"Good."

With a leap, Camry jumped back into Tasker's arms, trusting his gargoyle to catch him, which he did.

"What?" Tasker cupped Camry's ass with one hand and wound his other arm around his back. "Camry?"

Smirking, Camry stated, "You once told me that if I were to jump naked into your arms, you'd pin me to the wall and fuck us both stupid."

Tasker sucked in a harsh breath. "B-But . . . you're not ready."

"I'm ready," Camry assured, rocking his hips to grind his swiftly hardening prick against Tasker's abdominals. "Get your lube and show me that skill with your tail again, my gargoyle." Allowing his voice to drop to a husky purr, Camry ordered, "Open me up, make me come, then shove your dick in, peg my prostate, and make me come twice more as you claim your mate proper this time."

Even as Tasker roved his gaze over the shower, he asked, "Are you certain?"

"Never more certain of anything, Tasker." When Tasker met Camry's gaze again, he told him, "I want to feel you in the morning, my gargoyle. Can you do that for me?"

Tasker must have located the lube, for he released Camry's back in favor of grabbing it. "I can do that, my mate," he replied, using his thumb to pop it open. "I can do anything for you, Camry."

Then Tasker poured a liberal amount of slick onto the tip of his tail before sliding it into Camry's ass and reminding him of just how much control he had over his extra appendage.

As Camry had requested, Tasker tail-fucked him until he blew, only to replace that appendage with a much thicker one. Blissed out on endorphins, Camry welcomed the invasion, loving every sensation Tasker wrung from his body. When Tasker sank his canines back into his claiming scar, Camry damn near passed out.

Camry hummed as he enjoyed Tasker's gentle hands washing him, then drying him, and finally tucking him into bed. When Tasker spooned up behind him and pressed a kiss to his nape, Camry let out a deep sigh.

"Thank you, my gargoyle," Camry whispered, feeling content beyond anything he'd ever thought possible.

Camry heard Tasker murmur, "Thank you back, my mate."

With a smile on his lips, Camry drifted into a peaceful sleep, knowing that he would have this and more for all time.

ABOUT THE AUTHOR

Charlie started writing fantasy when she was eight, and after stumbling onto her first erotic romance at age nineteen, she realized her true calling. She now focuses on writing gay erotic romance, normally of the paranormal variety, with heroes of all kinds. With the help and support of her husband, Charlie finally fulfilled one of her life-long goals . . . move to acreage with her horses. You can often find her curled up with her laptop and a cup of tea or glass of wine, creating her next adventure. Charlie enjoys exploring the mountains of her new Oregon home on horseback, 4-wheeler, or motorcycle.

She can be reached at ch.richards2010@yahoo.com
Or visit her at www.charlie-richards.com.